SKINNY McCORD

HE GROPED BLINDLY FOR THE PROJECTED TREE.

Skinny Mc Cord.   *Frontispiece (Page 63)*

SKINNY McCORD

By

PERCY KEESE FITZHUGH

Author of

THE TOM SLADE BOOKS
THE ROY BLAKELEY BOOKS
THE PEE-WEE HARRIS BOOKS
THE WESTY MARTIN BOOKS

ILLUSTRATED BY
HOWARD L. HASTINGS

GROSSET & DUNLAP
PUBLISHERS   NEW YORK

CONTENTS

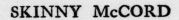

SKINNY McCORD

SKINNY McCORD

CHAPTER I

SKINNY LOSES SOMETHING

There was great excitement around the camp-fire. Skinny McCord had lost his compass. He had dropped it and it had rolled away, and all the boys were making a great show of helping him to find it. They did this not wholly from kindness.

Skinny was a sensitive boy and it gave his comrades great delight to see him embarrassed, as he always was when made the subject of group talk or the center of interest. Not that they would have hesitated a moment to assist Skinny. For they liked him immensely and would have done anything in the world for him. But they were a mirthful lot, these scouts of Temple Camp, and felt a certain bantering enjoyment in seeing him uneasy, as he always was when the spotlight was thrown on him. They liked that diffident way of his—that bashful

1

smile. This was his second summer at camp and still he was shy; he would probably always be shy. . . .

It was not much of a compass that he had lost; just a little tin affair. He was sorry that he had chosen to transfer it from one pocket to another, for now he found himself the star attraction of the camp-fire throng. "It—it isn't much good anyway," he said; "don't bother."

But they did bother. They had Skinny where they wanted him and they could not let the occasion go by. He would have to go through with this torture. He often suffered such torture at the hands of these scouts who would have knocked any one down who dared to harm him.

"Everybody hunt for Skinny's compass!" called Roy Blakeley. (He was easily the worst of the lot.) "Get out of the way," he said as he rolled Pee-wee Harris over on the ground, and made great pretense of scrutinizing the spot. "Don't sit around gaping when Skinny's compass is lost. Correct imitation of boy scouts hunting for a lost compass that didn't know which way it was rolling."

"Would you mind getting up, Uncle Jeb, so we can look under that log for Skinny Mc-

Cord?" said another boy. Poor Skinny looked almost frightened to see the old western trapper, master of woods lore in camp, smilingly arise while a dozen scouts searched under the log seat, to the accompaniment of a clamorous chorus.

"All fall to and hunt for Skinny's compass!"

"Hey, Skinny, we'll find it!"

"Go and get a couple of scoutmasters and a few councilors."

"Tell them Skinny McCord lost his compass."

"We'll form a posse," said Roy.

"Don't worry, Skinny, we'll find it."

"Everybody hunt for the compass of Skinny McCord."

"Sit still, Skinny; your thousands of friends will find it for you."

He sat still, his face as red as the end of the big iron poker which lay in the fire. He might have served as a model for a statue of embarrassment as he sat on his old grocery box fearfully contemplating the rumpus he had caused. Timidly he glanced at Councilor Barrows as if to assure that smiling official that he had not intended to interrupt the proceedings with all this hubbub.

In company Skinny never permitted himself

to occupy a whole seat. He sat on the edge of a chair or box or boat seat; this was the invariable sign of his embarrassment. "Sit back and make yourself at home, Skinny," they would say. But that was the one thing poor Skinny could never do—make himself at home. His getting into the scouts was the great thing in his young life and he had been in a sort of trance ever since. He had never got over the shock. They had told him that pretty soon he would be a patrol leader. His elevation to that height would certainly have killed him.

A scout from Indiana (one of those robust jolliers who enliven camps) jumped upon a rough seat, cupped his hands to his mouth and shouted like a fish pedler, "Ooooooh! Everybody! Scout McCord of Bridgeboro—First Bridgeboro Troop—has lost his compass! Come one, come all, and help find it!"

They were all crawling about on their hands and knees, fifty or more of them, upturning boxes and throwing camp stools about in hilarious exaggeration of helpfulness. And there sat poor Skinny smiling bashfully. If a pack of lions had suddenly taken it into their heads to roar their tribute to a kitten as a member of their family, the kitten's attitude would have been comparable to that of poor Skinny.

But the spasm of raillery was soon over. They were more concerned with Skinny's discomfiture than with finding the fugitive compass. And they did not find it; it had rolled gayly off and baffled all these trackers and pathfinders. Skinny did not let his uproarious comrades know how much he really did want to find it. He was even glad when the excitement was over. He hoped they would resume camp-fire yarns and forget all about it. He had suffered quite enough this agony of being in the public eye.

But the fire was burning low now and there were no more camp-fire yarns. There was a continuous exodus from the spot. Sitting there one might see scouts, singly and in groups, moving into the darkness, up the hill or along Cabin Lane or toward Tent Village, as they called it, to their quarters. Slowly the reflection of the fire in the lake near by diminished until there was nothing but a tiny red glow on the black water.

"So long, see you in the morning," was repeated again and again as patrols went their several ways off into the solemn stillness of the big scout community. It was more than a camp, this lakeside foundation started by Mr. John Temple; it was a sort of scout city in the

wilderness. One could be quite alone and un-
noticed there, if he so chose, even as one may
be a hermit in the metropolis.

Soon only half a dozen or so of the merry,
lolling throng remained, and these sat medi-
tating as they waited for the fire to die. There
were always a few to linger like this; a few
who had that gentle sentiment that likes to see
the old year go out, or watch beside a dying
fire. Old Uncle Jeb and Tom Slade, camp assistant, always waited to trample out the last
embers. With them sat two or three of the
older boys.

"Poor kid, it's a lot of fun to see him all
flustered," one said.

"He's even got a regular scout suit," said
another. "He drove down to Kingston with
Curry in his Ford and bought it and now he's
afraid to wear it. Somebody told me he's been
saving up for it ever since last summer. And
now he's afraid to wear it."

"Curry told me it's about forty-'leven sizes
too big," drawled lanky Brent Gaylong. "But
I s'pose Skinny figures on growing up to it.
Probably he means to wear it when he's
National Scout Commissioner. A scout has to
be prepared as I understand."

"Look out, you'll burn your shoe," said Tom.

"If *you* dressed more like a scout it wouldn't hurt you any."

"I have the soul of a scout," drawled Brent. "I don't need the tinseled regalia. What do you suppose would happen," he said meditatively after a pause, "if Skinny were to be awarded the Gold Cross and all the high dinkums of scouting were here to pull the presentation stuff to the plaudits of the multitude? What do you think he'd do if old man Temple made one of his speeches about him?"

"I think he'd drop dead," said Tom. "But Skinny is no coward; he's just bashful and sensitive."

"Huh, funny," mused Brent. "He doesn't seem to be any more at home with the Elks than when he first joined them."

"He's happy," said Tom.

"Thar's cowardly animals, and thar's timid animals," said old Uncle Jeb, "n' they ain't the same by no manner o' means. That thar youngster's all right, I reckon. On'y he's shy."

Two of those who had lingered went away; they were silhouetted as they passed the big lighted window of Benson Dormitory, then were swallowed by the darkness. Still the trio waited by the dying fire, silent, meditative. Tom was watching a particular patch of embers

as one by one little particles went out and the
tiny area of red diminished. He could have
stamped this out with one foot, but he took a
certain idle pleasure in waiting till it vanished
in the black night. "Why don't the Elks get
after Skinny about his new suit?" he mused
aloud.

"I suppose they don't know anything about
it," drawled Brent.

"Hmph, poor kid," said Tom.

CHAPTER II

Tom, Brent and Uncle Jeb were not the only persons who waited that night for the camp-fire to die. All unknown to each other two boys lingered in the darkness. One was a slim little fellow with big, staring eyes, a queer gnome of a boy, who stole out of the Elks patrol cabin and stood with his gaze fixed on the dying embers, listening and eagerly waiting for the last watchers to withdraw. He intended to steal back alone and search for his precious compass. For this little trinket meant more to him than he had been willing for that hilarious company to believe.

Now that he had at last achieved the glory of a real scout suit he could wear this little appurtenance dangling from his scout belt in the flaunting manner of Pee-wee Harris. In the store at Kingston he had bashfully tried this suit on (to the great amusement of his companion, Curry) and he had looked like a bolster in it. But no size seemed to fit him. Poor Skinny would never look trim. As he waited

9

there in the darkness, watching the last faint glow of the fire, he had not a little the appearance of an hour glass, with his belt drawn so absurdly tight that his clothing seemed to bulge above and below it.

The other boy who waited for the fire to die was not a scout. He sat on a rough bench up at the roadside just where the path led down through the woods into camp. Approaching along this road one reached a sign with an arrow pointing down into the woods and with the words *To Temple Camp* printed on it. A trail wound down the wooded slope to the sprawling scout community at the lakeside. At this point where the trail left the road stood the old bench and close by it a post surmounted by a huge letter-box where the rural carrier left the camp mail.

The spot was a pleasant loitering place as was evidenced by the many carved initials on the bench and the post. No part of the camp was visible from this spot though sometimes a little glint of silvery water was discoverable through the trees. But at night two distinct glowing areas could be seen from the wayside seat. Many a new scout had been fooled by these. It was one of the popular jokes of camp to take a new arrival up to the road at night, and then send him forth to find the northernmost glow, which was only the reflection of the camp-fire in the distant lake. Even so good a scout as Bert Winton, who was a Vermont Eagle, had gone hiking down into the dark woods in search of this fire and had gone clear around the camp and come out up at the end of the lake where Tenderfoot Cove is, only to see the glow reduced to a little glinting patch on the water.

The boy who was not a scout had come along the road looking for the camp. At Leeds, the nearest village, he had been told where to turn down into the woods. But now that he had reached the spot he hesitated, for the two bright areas down there in the woods told him that the camp people were still about. It was his intention to enter the camp unseen. He was very weary and was not averse to sitting on the bench and waiting. Now and then he glanced furtively up and down the dark road as if fearful that he might be discovered, and once when an auto sped by, throwing a momentary glare over the spot, he cringed and breathed quickly.

He was about sixteen, this boy, and tall of stature with a litheness about him which suggested the cautious stealth of an animal. His eyes were gray and large, but he kept them

half closed and used them with a kind of darting agility. When he arose and stepped across
the road for a better look at the glowing areas,
there was a certain elasticity in his step, a
silent springiness, very suggestive of wild life
and extraordinarily graceful. He laid his hands
against his hips and narrowed his eyes in
studious concentration on those distant spots
of light. It was a fine, unconscious posture.

The path of least resistance for a boy's hands
at this moment would have been his trousers
pockets, but the trousers worn by this boy had
no pockets. They were gingham trousers and
afforded their wearer not one single carrying
facility. This boy had grown used to pocket-
less trousers and accustomed himself to that
picturesque way of standing with his hands
against his hips.

For several minutes he gazed steadily at
those distant glowing patches. His narrowed
eyes became steely in this concentration. A
fine, inspiring figure of a scout, baffled and
yet resolved, he made as he stood there. Suddenly some little creature of the woodland
made a sound in its nightly prowling and the
boy turned with lightning rapidity, listening
fearfully. Then he resumed his study of the
distant patches of light. He was vivisecting

them at long distance, comparing the flickering movements one with another.

"I'll be— Those aren't two fires," said he. "There's only one. The other's just a reflection. The two of them move alike."

It was not so bad for a boy who was not a scout. Still, when this boy set about doing a thing he usually succeeded. The very night before he had essayed to do a daring thing, a dreadful thing. And he had succeeded.

CHAPTER III

EARS THAT HEAR

It was a desperate business, but he had succeeded—so far. He was not going to jeopardize his success now by an ill-considered move. So he resolved to rest on the bench till the last distant flicker disappeared and he could feel certain that every one in camp had retired. Then he would follow the path down through the woods.

He removed his hat and took an empty cigarette box from inside the crown. There were no cigarettes left in it, but a certain devilish instinct of caution had prompted him to save the little pasteboard folder with removable matches that had accompanied his forbidden purchase. Then he took off a shoe and withdrew from it a damp and soiled slip of paper containing a memorandum which he read by the light of a match. *Martha Norris Memorial Cabins. Up path from fire turn left—second cabin.* He knew the words by heart, but scanned them finally before crumpling the paper and throwing it away.

As he dropped it under the bench he saw a little square of white lying on the ground and picking it up found it to be an unopened letter. It was close to one of the legs of the bench and almost at the foot of the post supporting the mail box. He struck another match and read the typewritten address on the envelope: *Temple Camp, Black Lake, Greene Co., New York.* In the corner was an imprint: *Bently's Family Hotel, Wave Crest City, Florida.*

He now made a discovery which was destined to give a turn to his fortunes and start an altogether singular series of adventures. He found that the heavy dew had dampened the envelope and melted the glue of the flap so that the envelope lay limp and open in his hand. He could not forbear to examine a missive which lay thus exposed. The thought occurred to him that the letter could not have lain long on the ground without being discovered by those who frequented the spot. It had probably been brought by the rural carrier that very afternoon and dropped by the messenger who had emptied the box to take its contents down to camp. In the dim light of his few remaining matches, he read the letter.

Wave Crest City, Fla.,
June 27th, 1927.

Board of Councilors,
Temple Camp,
Black Lake, N. Y.
Gentlemen:

This is to notify you that my son, Danville Bently, who was to have spent the month of July at your camp will not be able to begin his vacation with you until August second. He is to accompany his mother and myself to Europe.

We are closing our place here for the summer season to travel abroad and I have taken the liberty of assuring our boy that the reservation made for him for July (for which check was sent to cover) may be shifted to August without prejudice to your summer arrangements.

He is looking forward with high anticipations to his promised month at your famous camp and we have arranged for him to return with his older brother on a steamer which will arrive in New York on August first, so that his trip with us may not interfere with his scouting activities.

Will you kindly wire me upon receipt of this whether the check forwarded in recent communication may be applied to accommodation for August instead of July? If that is satisfactory he will report on August second.

I sincerely hope that this will be agreeable to you as he would suffer a very keen disappointment if compelled to forego this first season at a scout camp.

Very truly yours,

Roswell T. Bently.

As he followed the path down into the woods he had no other thought in regard to this letter than to see that it was delivered into the proper

hands. He knew well enough how he was to
accomplish this without making his presence
known to these strangers. The faintest glow
of the distant fire still burned and by this tiny
beacon he saw that to reach the site of the camp-
fire he must leave the beaten path. He now
began to pass isolated cabins, the scattered
advance guard of the growing camp. They
were all in darkness, but in one he heard
laughter and singing. Now he passed a row
of tents; there was a dim light in one of them
and a figure silhouetted on the canvas. As he
passed the light went out. He moved silently,
cautiously pausing now and again. There was
no sign of life.

Presently he was shockingly made aware of
the need of stealth. Pausing before a cabin in
front of which was planted a staff with a white
pennant he saw a figure appear suddenly in the
doorway.

"No, you don't," said the apparition.

"Did he get away with it?" some one within
asked.

"Not so you'd notice it," said the figure in
the doorway.

"What's the idea?" the newcomer asked.

"The idea is you didn't get away with it,"
laughed the boy in the doorway. "Just keep

away from that pennant.'' And he disappeared within.

Here was a strange business. They evidently slept with one ear open at Temple Camp. But why should they think he intended to take something? Why should they suspect him? Was there anything about him that enabled strangers to discern his secret? At all events he must be careful in this uncanny place.

CHAPTER IV

BY THE DEAD FIRE

Of course no one suspected him of trying to steal. He had just had a glimpse of a little nocturnal game that was popular in camp. Whoever could remove this pennant was welcome to it and might plant it in front of his patrol cabin. These midnight raids were very common and not infrequently successful. Our stealthy visitor had chanced to pause before the pennant cabin.

He now came to the main body of the camp and saw the whole expanse of the dark lake with the great bulk of wooded hills beyond. He glanced about at the cluster of rustic buildings, the main pavilion, the storehouse and cooking shack, the "eats" pavilion, Administration Shack. Cautiously (for now he was fearful of the slightest sound) he approached the lake and stood on the float looking off across the black water. Close by him the rocking boats knocked one against another; there was the metallic sound of clanking oar-locks now and then. How strange seemed all these evidences of

19

life when deserted and wrapped in darkness!

The diving board pointed out into the lake like a big, ghostly finger. Slanting upward as it did, it seemed to be pointing at the precipitous hills across the lake which cast their inverted shadow in the water, making the dark surface still darker. At night there seemed always to be two shades of blackness on that enclosed lake, caused by the vast shadow of the rugged heights beyond. Scouts had tried to row out to where this deeper gloom in the water began, but they could never find it.

The prowling stranger examined one of the boats to see if it was locked. He lifted the chain as gingerly as one would handle a snake. No, the boats were not locked. He might take one, if he could find the oars, and row across and baffle pursuit among those wilderness-clad hills. He could push the boat back into the lake again and they would just think it had drifted away from its mooring. He was altogether too clever, this strange boy.

But just now he had business in the camp; then he would consider how best to proceed on his fugitive way. This was a ticklish matter that he had now to transact. Then all would be well. So far he believed he had done well —if you call it doing well to do what he had done. At least good luck had smiled upon him.

He must now find the camp-fire spot. From this point (according to the only hint he had) he would see a hill and up that hill *to the left,* would be the Martha Norris Memorial Cabins. But how to find and awaken a particular sleeper in that group was a puzzle. If these boy scouts (he called them boy scouts notwithstanding that he was himself a boy) were all like the one who had appeared in the cabin doorway, he would have to practice superhuman stealth. He could do that. He had, in perverted form, every physical quality dear to scouting.

If he had not been absorbed by very pressing business, he might have spared a moment to flatter himself that not many boys could prowl around a sleeping scout camp undiscovered. He was beating them at their own game. But his only thought about this remote scout community was that it was to serve his purpose. Two days previously he had never thought about it. Then he had had an inspiration. And two days hence he would forget that there was such a place as Temple Camp.

He found the camp-fire spot, a circle of low masonry, about eight inches high and ten feet in diameter. It was well removed from the

nearest building. As he looked at it, it reminded him of a tiny circus ring. It was all
strewn with gray ashes and charred bits of
log. He was in the very heart of Temple Camp.
For as the camp had grown larger and extended up the wooded hillside away from the
lake, this nightly gathering place had come to
be more than just a camp-fire. Scouts who
seldom met at other times, met here. It was
the market-place of camp.

The roaring blaze which nightly painted its
counterpart in the dark lake, embodied the very
essence of scouting. And the romance of this
enchanted spot lingered in the daytime when
only ashes remained within the stone circle, and
only upturned boxes and ramshackle benches
and pieces of canvas lay about outside, giving
silent testimony of the throngs that gathered
there when the day was done. The roaring
fire is a feature of every camp. At Temple
Camp it was an institution.

But our stealthy visitor had no sentiment
about this merry ceremonial of scouting. He
approached the hallowed spot with caution and
glanced about. There seemed to be a hill, or
spreading knoll, rising from the neighborhood,
but he could see no cabins on this rising ground.
There was a trail, however, which seemed to

come from around the cooking shack and peter
out on this slight eminence. He hardly knew
what to do. He had not fancied the camp to
be anything like this, a community made up of
cabin groups and rustic avenues and tiny isolated abodes far removed from the body of
the original camp. It was like a little city with
tiny suburbs. Even with the information he
had, he was hunting for a needle in a haystack.

His foot caught in a loop of rope attached
to a square of old tent canvas on which several
scouts had sprawled. He stumbled, fell over a
bench, scrambled to his feet, and was instantly
aware of a dark figure on the opposite side of
the circle. It seemed to have risen simultan-
eously with him, almost like his shadow. He
was startled, every nerve on edge. Was this
another of those uncanny beings appearing to
challenge him? The dark figure said not a
word, only stared at him.

CHAPTER V

FACE TO FACE

For a few moments the stranger scrutinized the figure. It moved, and he seemed relieved.

"That you, Tiny?" he ventured hesitatingly.

"It's—it's *Danny!*" said the other, aghast.

"*Hsh,* not so loud. Yes, it's Danny. I'm in luck."

He stepped across the circle and put his arm around the younger boy. "What are you doing here—this time of night?" he whispered.

"I was hunting for my compass. They were making fun of me so I came back alone to hunt for it. Did they—Danny, did they let you out?"

"*Shh*—ut up. No, I gave them the slip. I hiked it all the way here to see you. I'm on my way—now don't get excited and don't talk loud."

"You mean—you—mean you *escaped?*"

"Yep, and you're going to pay me back for licking Dick Kinney. Don't you know how you said you would?"

24

"Yes, only I'm scared."

"I'm the one to be scared—only I'm not."

"Yes, but Danny," Skinny pleaded as he nervously gripped the other's shirt with both hands, "listen—Danny—" (he almost pulled the shirt up over the other's belt in his nervous excitement) "you, you stepped right in the ashes and now you'll make tracks."

"You little devil of a boy scout," laughed the taller boy in a good-humored whisper. "Come on, where can we go and talk? This blamed place sleeps with its ears open."

"Are they—Danny, are they coming after you?" Skinny asked in panic fright. "Are they coming here, Danny?"

"Not to-night, kid."

"But to-morrow—Danny?"

"I'll be gone before to-morrow."

"Yes, but they'll get you, Danny," Skinny said, jerking in a panic of fear at the shirt he still gripped. "I know how you licked Dick Kinney, but——"

"Come ahead, where can we talk, kid?"

"Maybe they don't know you've got a brother here, hey?" Skinny said hopefully.

"Naah, they don't know that. They're a bunch of yimps."

"Yes, but—all right, come on up this way."

You would never have supposed that the diffident, bashfully smiling little fellow who had blushed scarlet at the rumpus he had caused at camp-fire was the same as he who now hurried silently up the wooded hillside away from the main body of camp, expressing nervous excitement in every look and move. Little did his scout comrades know of the fire that burned in the soul of this forlorn little scout whose quaint discomfiture they so much enjoyed.

"Come on up here," he breathed excitedly, looking fearfully back toward the area of peril. "Now I'm glad they jollied me—you bet; I'm glad I went back there. Come on up this way and don't speak when we go past that cabin. There's a scout in there that's got the *one eye* cup. That's for sleeping with one eye open. It don't mean that exactly—shhh. He's the one makes fun of me, because I didn't have a scout suit——"

"He'd sleep with both eyes black if I was here," said Danny. This was quite a boast, but I dare say he would have made it good.

"Hsh, we have to be good and scared of *that* feller."

It was no wonder that this dubious brother treated Skinny with a kind of protective kindness. Such an odd, likable, temperamental little bundle of nerves he seemed, when aroused. It was his fate never to be at his best in public; his sadder fate to be at his very best with this fugitive adventurer when secrecy was imperative. A queer little hobgoblin of a boy he seemed without one single evidence of the scout in his appearance.

He led the way up the hill till their progress was interrupted by an old railroad cut, which at that point was so overgrown that it seemed a natural hollow. Clambering down the side with the aid of trees and brush, Skinny stood triumphantly beside a tiny shanty which had once been a shelter for a switchman. It was now quite fallen to pieces, but its board roof had been propped up, and the dense brush that tumbled over it effectually concealed it and kept it from leaking too freely. As a romantic retreat there was much to be said for it. Skinny had discovered it and made it his own; it was his private retreat.

Within there was nothing but a shelf and an old red lantern hanging on a rusty nail. But there was oil inside the lantern which Skinny had once fetched thither in a tomato can. The smell of this lantern when lighted was like unto no stench that ever assailed human nostrils. To this remote refuge Skinny was wont to re-

pair when he wanted to pretend that he was a
pioneer, and when the banter at camp was too
vociferous for him.

The very sight of this place was a relief to
Danny, and he perched on the shelf while
Skinny lighted the lantern. "Listen here,
Tiny," said he. "Do you remember when you
was just a little bit of a shaver and you said I
was half a brother——"

"I didn't mean it that way—honest——"

"I know you didn't, you thick little dub. Do
you remember how pop told you I was *half-
brother,* not half a brother? Then when Dick
Kinney said you were only about a quarter of
a brother and he took your ball away, do you
remember how I landed him one? Knocked
him goofy? And you said you'd pay me back?"

"Sure, I do, Danny, only——"

"Naah, there's no *only* about it kid. I got a
letter from pop and he said how he sent you
fifteen dollars—I got it at Blythedale. He says
when I get out next year he hopes I'll work.
Get a picture of me sticking around a reformatory till next year! Listen, kid, they had me out
fixing a grape-vine over an arbor, tying it up.
They even give me a ball of cord, the poor
simps! So listen to what I did. I picked out a
nice long stem of grape-vine—*a nice long one.*

Nice and long—and thick. And that one I didn't wind around the new arbor; I only laid it nice and easy on top. You'd think it was all wound up like the other branches and things but it wasn't. Camouflage! About—oh thirty or forty feet, maybe, of the cord I rolled up and put in my pocket. Of course those wise guys had to have their ball of cord back.

"Well—don't get scared. Any one would think it was *you* doing this. Well, as——"

"I'm not scared, only——"

"Wait till you hear, kid; it's good. It was so easy I'm sorry now I didn't go and say good-by to Punkhead; he's got charge of my floor."

Skinny's expression seemed to say that he thought it just as well his half-brother had not done that.

"After supper I did my little job carrying ice in from the ice-house and dumping it in the box in the outside pantry. Then I went up-stairs with the ice-tongs—don't laugh at them, kid, they're simps. At Blythedale Home all those managers need is a mother's care."

Skinny was far from laughing at this dreadful recital.

"So I put the ice-tongs under my mattress. Then I stayed awake till I heard the church clock in Blythedale ring two. Then I tied the ice-tongs to the cord and dropped it down out of the window and pulled up the grape-vine and tied it good and fast to the shutter hinge. Zip goes the fillum. I wrote on a piece of paper, *Get two hunks of ice to-morrow so you can cool down. So long.* Then I slid down the grape-vine.

"I had some stuff I kept from my supper and I got as far as Tonley's Corners before it got light. Then I hid under a lunch wagon that was all boarded up till last night and then I started hiking again. I grubbed some eats and got a hitch with a wop in a flivver—he can't even speak English. So here I am and it's just exactly fifty-one miles from Blythedale Home to Temple Camp and you're looking great, kid.

"All I want is that fifteen bucks so I can get a good start. I was thinking I'd bang down to New York and get a job on a ship. But I can't chase around in these blamed calico things, I'll get pinched *sure.* Say, kid, how about that lake; what's on the other side? Could I get through to Catskill that way without going on a road? Hsh—*listen.*"

"That's only a bird house that kinder creaks in a tree when the wind blows. Collie Edwards put it there; he's a Star Scout."

"Didn't you hear voices—men?"

"No, it wasn't voices, Danny. Now I'm sorry I bought a scout suit and some things, because I haven't got that money. I only got eleven cents of it now—that's all I got."

"You got a *suit* and things?" Danny asked, aghast.

"Yes, because I never had any and they kept saying how I have to have one, because I'm a scout. Honest Danny, I'm sorry."

The elder boy sat on the shelf dangling his legs and contemplating his half-brother in a daze.

"If you're mad I don't blame you, but it isn't my fault," said Skinny.

"*Now* what am I going to do? *Now* what in blazes am I going to do?" was all that Danny could say.

"Could—maybe you could wear the suit," Skinny ventured. "Then people wouldn't know you got out of a reform school. You can have it if you want it; anyway, it's too big for me. Curry had to laugh at me in it. They don't make them like the shape I am."

Something in this last wistful remark touched the brother. Even in his troubled preoccupation he reached out and ruffled the younger boy's hair. "Who's Curry? Did you

tell him what I did to Kinney for making fun
of you?''

''No, because he's a nice fellow; he's an assistant scoutmaster. They all kinder laugh at me,
but just the same I'm good friends with them.''

''I couldn't pay railroad fares with a scout
suit, kid.''

''Maybe you could hook a ride, you're so
smart. I guess you could do it if you wanted to
like the way you do 'most everything. I never
told them about you 'cause I couldn't.''

Danny only gazed at him in a kind of blank
abstraction. Sometimes great anxiety finds relief in a trifling, irrelevant act. ''Here,'' said
he impulsively, ''here's a letter I picked up.
You better chuck it on the counter or somewhere. Who's Danville Bently; did you ever
hear of him?''

''There's lots of fellers come here I never
heard of,'' said Skinny. ''Anyway, most of
them don't bother with me; even my own patrol
doesn't.''

''Well that's a guy that isn't coming,'' said
Danny. ''He's giving them a stall till August.
Maybe I might be him, huh?'' He laughed
at the absurdity of the idea. ''Hide inside
of somebody else. Ever hear of that? Go
ahead, read it, it's open.''

It was then that Skinny, all in innocence, made a remark much deeper than his wit had intended. He was great for blundering remarks. His sober and literal answers were one of the jokes of camp. "You can't hide inside of a scout if you're *not* a scout; you can't do that," he said, looking wide eyed at his half-brother.

Danny reached forward and ruffled his hair again. Skinny was accustomed to that. It was done to him twenty times a day.

CHAPTER VI

IN THE DIM LIGHT

"Just the same I think I can," said Danny. "And just the same I think I will."

It was in just that casual, reckless spirit that Danny McCord first proposed the impersonation of Danville Bently at Temple Camp. He thought of it as a joke, and then the idea captivated him. He was amused by Skinny's terror at the very thought. It would be hard to say just when or how he passed from humorous to serious consideration of this preposterous enterprise. But once decided, the terrified Skinny could not dissuade him. He had unbounded confidence in himself, this fugitive boy, and he knew nothing whatever about scouting.

Skinny's disbursement of his funds had dashed the brother's hopes. He had not the wherewithal to make good his escape. But he might remain at camp, pretending to be this boy whose coming was postponed for a month. It was such a bit of daredevil effrontery as left Skinny speechless with fear and apprehension.

"You'll—you'll be sorry," was all he could

stammer, as he stood, a pathetic little figure, in the dim glow of the smelly old red lantern. "Remember what I said when you were going to take Mr. Burt's Ford for a joy ride—remember what I said."

"You said you wouldn't tell," said Danny, ruffling the little fellow's hair in that fraternal way he had. I dare say the best thing about this dubious brother was his condescending but genuine fondness for Skinny. He trusted him. "And you didn't either, because you're a little brick."

"Even if they had *killed* me," said Skinny emphasizing the word with nervous tension; "even then I wouldn't tell. Even if they had *killed* me!"

"Don't get excited, Tiny," Danny laughed, pulling Skinny toward him and unclenching the little fellow's fist; he had even dug his nails into the palms of his hands. "Sure you didn't tell. And am I blaming you because they chased me up to Blythdale? And I'm not sore because you haven't got any money, kid."

"No, but now you're going to get into more trouble. If you stay here they'll come and find you."

"Not if I'm Danville Bently, kid. Do you want me to start away from here without any money? I was going to go and get a job on a ship. How can I do that now? This is my only chance, Teeny-weeny; don't worry."

"That's what you said before and you went to reform school."

"And I got away from there, too."

Skinny gazed at his half-brother, admiringly, trustful, but panic-stricken. "You're going to get in a lot of trouble, Danny," he said in fearful agitation. "I know you licked Kinney and he was bigger than you, and you climbed over the fence of Garrett's Field with me so I could peek under the circus tent, and I know you got away from the Home——"

"Hey, don't call it a home, kid."

"I don't blame you for it," said Skinny loyally, "only now you're going to get found out, because being a scout is—kinder you got to know all about it, how they do and everything. I know you're all the time laughing at them, Danny, but anyway, you got to know how they do and everything." His panic apprehension was pitiful, but Danny only laughed.

"Give us the letter, kid, and I'll burn it up. Now I tell you what you do; you're going to be a bully little kid and stand by me like you always did; hey?"

"Yes, but——"

"You chase down and get that primer or whatever you call it, that you kids use."

"That's the Scout Handbook, it ain't a primer."

"Yere, you get that. How much oil is there in this blamed magic lantern; will it burn a couple of hours? Gee, it makes your face look red kid——"

"I gained two pounds, Danny, up here."

"*Yere?* The blamed thing makes us look like a couple of Indians——"

"Now I got a thought, Danny. A red light means danger. There's danger waiting for you Danny."

"All right, tell it to wait. Now you chase down and see if you can sneak in and get your book and your new suit and bring them up here. Bring anything you've got that you don't need. Go on, chase yourself now and if you wake them up I'll know you're a ham scout. That gosh blamed bird-house—are you sure that's what it is?"

They both listened. In the stillness of the night was a creaking sound followed by another like the breaking of twigs. "Is it somebody walking?" Danny whispered.

"I never heard it just like that before,"

Skinny whispered in terror. "Shall we look out?"

"If I start running, don't you say who I am," said Danny. "They might have dogs out, I don't know. *Shh—ut up.*"

Skinny McCord had many times been hurt by boys who meant him no harm. Occasionally his pride had been touched when bantering comrades had referred to his humble origin and poor abode in Bridgeboro. But when Danny mentioned the possibility of dogs being on his trail, something in that narrow chest of little Skinny McCord rose and he flushed with anger. Instinctively he felt what officialdom does not feel, the degrading character of setting a beast to catch a human being. Truly, indeed, human nature can sink no lower than this. To the powers of law enforcement belongs the contemptible distinction which places them below the level of the vilest criminal.

"They wouldn't do that!" whispered Skinny. "Oh, wouldn't they, though!"

"I'll do what you want me to," Skinny said.

CHAPTER VII

DARK PLANS

There came a time when they said of Skinny that he had been frightened into participation in his half-brother's bizarre and daring plan. But that was not true of him. He tried, as we have seen, to dissuade Danny. When the worst came to the worst and he knew that he could not dissuade him, he was loyal. He was loyal in a dastardly business.

This wonderful big brother of his could not teach him anything in the matter of stealth; he was a little demon at that. He had accustomed himself to stepping carefully and making no noise in the days when he went barefoot in the slummy east end of Bridgeboro whence he had emanated one day to stare wide eyed at the scouts practicing archery. There happened to be a vacancy in Connie Bennett's patrol (Elks), so they took him in. He was their mascot. They didn't even mind his not having a scout suit. He had a winsome smile when they jollied him and they liked him immensely. He was not only glad, but proud to run on errands.

When the McCords moved to Bridgeboro and hired three rooms in Corkscrew Alley down near the marsh that bordered the river, Danny was not with them. He had already taken his departure, under escort, to Blythedale Boys' Home, which he was right in saying was not a home at all. He had been sent thither because of his escapade with Mr. Burt's Ford, though this had by no means been his first escapade. But it was the crucial one. So the scouts of the First Bridgeboro Troop, of which Skinny was an obscure and lowly member, had never seen the enterprising Danny. His colorful career came to a halt in Irontown and soon afterward the hapless family moved to Bridgeboro, where Mr. McCord had secured a job in the paper mill. Danny's mother was dead and Skinny was the child of Mr. McCord's second wife. Whatever else may be said of Danny, he had always afforded Skinny all the sturdy advantages of a big brother.

Skinny missed him when he moved to Bridgeboro. The hoodlums down in Corkscrew Alley called him *Owleyes* and *Jumbo* and other piquant appellations. Once or twice he was moved to tell them that things would be different when Danny returned. When he got in with the scouts he never mentioned Danny. He had too much pride and these strange, wonderful boys of the upper world would not understand. They would not appreciate the knock-out blow administered to the unhappy Kinney. And now, at last, when Skinny had attained to the glory of a real scout suit, here was this brother come to Temple Camp, a fugitive, and with all his wonted assurance proposing a scheme for hiding which struck poor Skinny dumb with terror.

Silently he sped through the woods back to camp and stealthily, ever so stealthily, up to the Martha Norris Memorial Cabins, where his troop was quartered that season. A splendid organization was the First Bridgeboro Troop, with four full patrols, and they held sway in these four cabins which represented one of the camp endowments. In the Elks' cabin all was still.

With every nerve on edge, Skinny crept to the rustic lockers at the end of the building. He was so fearful that he jerked his foot up in nervous excitement as he turned the key of his own locker. He paused after the slight click, listening. His heart beat like a trip-hammer. No sound, no stir. Only the audible breathing of Vic Norris. One of the other boys turned over and settled down in deeper slumber.

Somewhere outside an owl hooted. Skinny stood stark still.

The plaguey hinges! He eased the swing of the locker door as he opened it inch by inch. There was his old pasteboard suit-case; he was the only boy in the patrol who had not a duffel bag. On top of it lay the bundle containing his scout suit and hat just as he had brought the treasured purchase back from Kingston. He had not dared to wear this flaunting regalia nor even to tell his patrol about it. He did not know whether or not they knew about it. Would the paper rustle as he lifted the bundle? No; he lifted it out carefully. Then he opened his suit-case and got his Handbook. So far, so good. Softly he closed the door and locked it. Then with his precious Handbook and the bundle he crept stealthily over to the trail which led up through the woods.

Now his heart beat more easily. Action is always stimulating, and being launched on this perilous business it was not so hard to go ahead. He had not done much so far, but what he had done had been successful. He had done what Danny had told him to do and it had been easy. It seemed to Skinny that this was a dreadful thing his brother was about to attempt, but Danny must know what he was about.

"Why it's going to be a cinch," his brother assured him when he had donned the suit; it fitted him much better than it fitted poor Skinny. When he tossed the hat on, he looked like a scout indeed and poor Skinny was even moved to feel a certain pride in him. He was a fine looking boy, there was no denying that, with an easy nonchalance about him that was captivating.

"You—you won't be a really truly scout," Skinny warned him. The warning seemed to include a confession that Danny did look like one. "And what are you going to do when he comes—that other feller?"

"I'll be on my way," said Danny lightly.

"You'll be using up the money that's going to pay his board, too," Skinny said.

The answer did not comfort him. "Sure, he'll be out of luck," said Danny.

Skinny gazed at this daring brother of his in mingled admiration and terror. "Will you —Danny, will you—if I get fifteen dollars, will you *not* do it?"

"Where would you get fifteen bucks, kid? You should worry," he added. "Let's take a look at that book. Does it tell all about it and everything? How you drill and everything?"

"*Now you see,* you don't know anything

about it," Skinny said excitedly, in a pitiable
way of triumph. "They don't drill at all; they
track and stalk and all like that, and win merit
badges, and all like that. Now you're going to
get in trouble." He clenched his little hands
nervously and almost cried as he spoke.
"You're going to get in trouble Danny.
They're smart, scouts are, and they'll find out.
Just because *I'm* not so smart and they make
fun of me like; and just because *I* can't do all
the things they do, you needn't think they're
not smart. That's where you're all the time
wrong, you think boy scouts——"

"Who makes fun of you?" Danny asked
with a queer scrutiny in his eyes.

"Now you're going to get into scraps, too,"
poor Skinny said. "You're going to call them
kids and everything. Even if they make fun
of me they're not mad at me."

There was a grim look in Danny's eyes and
a menacing sneer in his voice as he said, *"Is—
that—so!"* In the lowering comment was real
feeling for Skinny and a high contempt for
Temple Camp and all its scouts.

"You should worry, kid," he said. "Go on
back and go to bed. All you've got to do is
not notice me. Don't be coming around. Act
just like if you didn't know me. All I want to

do is just lay low for three or four days; I'll get away with it that long, don't worry. If you had the money I'd beat it, but I can't bang out of here without a red, and that bunch after me. What am I going to do? I know what's troubling you, kid. You think it's kind of like stealing, using up that what's-his-name's board money. You're a little brick, kiddo. But I'll only be here two or three days. And when he gets here next month—why these guys won't know till then there was anything phony about me! And *you* won't be hooked up with it at all. Now trot along and turn in, Tiny, old pal."

"Won't I see you any more after you go away from here? Maybe you'll go all the way around the world on a ship, hey?"

"*Suuuuure,* you'll see me again. And you'll get paid back for your suit too. Don't I line up pretty nice as a boy scout. How do you do that—what is it, a salute they've got?" He wriggled his thumb against his ear in a funny way and laughed at Skinny and gave him an affectionate shove. "Go on back now or you'll be walking in your sleep," said he. "And whatever you do, don't let on when you see me again."

"I can look at you, can't I?" said poor Skinny.

CHAPTER VIII

STEALTH

Well, if it was for only two or three days it would not be so bad, poor Skinny reflected as he went back through the darkness. Still his conscience troubled him and he was beside himself with fear. The only gleam of light he saw in this sorry business was that Danny did have a way of succeeding in the things he undertook. He trusted Danny to avert the catastrophe which would naturally ensue in such a daring and perilous business.

He hoped that during those dreadful two or three days the scouts at camp would not overstep their prerogative of banter where he was concerned. Or at least that Danny might not see them in full swing with their raillery. The historic Kinney of Irontown had got over the licking that Danny had given him. But poor Skinny had never got over it.

As he wandered, fearful and conscience-stricken, down the wooded slope a thought came to him. There was a rich boy in camp, Helmer Clarkson. That boy wanted a canoe and had

46

tried for the Hiawatha Prize—a fine canoe to
win which a scout must swim across the lake.
Helmer had started (according to rule) with
a rowboat escort, and like many another hope-
ful candidate had returned in the boat. So
Helmer had decided to fall back on the less
heroic plan of asking his father to buy him a
canoe. If he had not already done this, then
Skinny had a plan. He would swim across the
lake, win the canoe, and sell it to Helmer Clarkson. Then he would give the money to his erring brother.

He knew the camp people would regard him
contemptuously for selling a prize, but at least
he could help Danny, and put an end to this
dreadful thing that Danny was doing. All this
might be done immediately—the next morning.
The only difficulty would be that his comrades
would laugh at him as soon as he proposed the
heroic enterprise. Alas, they would not know
how heroic it was! They would make a great
joke of his trying for a prize—especially this
prize. They would decline to accompany him
with a boat. They would probably tell him, as
they had so many times told him, that if he had
to be taken into the boat it would probably sink
it. Skinny weighed sixty-four pounds, not
counting his heart, which weighed tons just now.

Well, he thought as he trudged along, if
Danny could do such wonderful (albeit dreadful) things, he, Skinny could do this. And it
would straighten everything out. Perhaps he
could even do it before Danny presented himself to the powers in Administration Shack
and signed up. That would be between ten and
eleven in the morning. He wondered if Helmer
Clarkson had any ready money; surely he must
have some. Fifteen dollars was all that Danny
had demanded. He would sell the prize canoe
to Clarkson for fifteen dollars. Well, that was
settled and things were not so bad.

As he passed down through the dark woods,
he thought of his fugitive brother hiding in
that little dank switchman's shanty. What
would be the first thing he would do in the
morning? Thus preoccupied with his thoughts,
Skinny found himself approaching the cabin
before which the white pennant flew. In there
they would be sleeping with one eye open, as
the saying is. If he could—if he only *could*—
"lift" that pennant. What a glory for the
Elks! It would raise him in their esteem; they
might take him seriously. Then perhaps they
would listen when he talked about trying for
the Hiawatha Prize. He was elated; he believed that the whole situation was in his

SKINNY STARTED RUNNING WITH THE WHITE PENNANT.

Skinny McCord.

hands; Danny, all unknown to the camp, might be on his way in the morning. This whole business was not so bad after all.

Never in all his trembling little life had Skinny moved with such stealth and caution as when he now approached that coveted pennant. He was about to try to do what Warde Hollister had failed to do; what Ellis Carway (who was an Eagle) had failed to do. He retreated a few yards, and sat down on a stump. He knew that he was out of his sphere, that this sort of thing was not expected of him. He felt that he was intruding into the heroic field where he had no business. He removed his shoes, tied the laces together, and hung the shoes around his neck. They were almost worn out; you could have stuck a finger through the soles.

Now, trembling in every nerve, he approached the cabin. The door stood ajar. He advanced a pace and paused listening. No sound. He took another step. No sound. He could reach out now and lift the staff. He paused, fearful to move. Straining his eyes he looked all about the staff. Then, ever so cautiously, he stooped, and shuddered as the clasp on his belt clinked. He felt all around on the ground, for he had heard scouts speak of cord attached to the staff and tied to the arm of some drowsy slacker on his cot. That was not considered good scouting, but it had been done.

But here there was no cord; these unknown scouts were playing the game right. The usual way with the patrol holding the white pennant was to sleep in turns, with one scout always awake to listen. In a full patrol no one scout would have to remain awake very long.

Skinny stood up and with trembling hand reached out and grasped the staff. Still no sound. There was a cricket chirping and he wished it would keep still. He had heard of rocks laid against the staff so that when it was lifted one would fall upon another. But nothing happened as he slowly raised the staff up, up, up——

What a queer little goblin of a boy he seemed, as he reached one foot far forward so as to cover all the ground he could with every pace. With each grotesque straining of a leg his face unconsciously assumed an aspect of demoniac fear. Then all of a sudden he started to run, his shoes flapping back and forth against his chest and shoulders like an outlandish bulky necklace. He held the white pennant in his trembling hand.

He had done it!

CHAPTER IX

FOR DANNY

He would have been proud of his achievement in any case, but he was doubly elated now, for it simplified the matter of Danny. With this "really and truly" scouting triumph to his credit, the Elks could not take him otherwise than seriously. They would escort him in his swim for the Hiawatha Prize and perhaps that very next morning Danny, his secret hero, would be on his way. The criminal and dangerous character of what Danny was going to do at Temple Camp impressed Skinny, but his conscience was not troubled about Danny's final exploit at the reform school.

When he reached the Elks' cabin, he found his patrol leader, Connie Bennett, waiting for him. It was well that he returned with the white pennant for this saved him the embarrassment of explaining his absence. The white pennant was always an excuse. It was a midnight passport even with the powers of Administration Shack.

"*I got it, I got it!*" he said excitedly. "*Look what I got!*"

"You little demon," said Connie. "So that's what you went after."

"*I got it, I got it!*" was all that Skinny could say.

"They didn't chase you?"

"They didn't hear me—even."

Connie softly closed the cabin door so as not to awaken the sleepers and together he and Skinny stood outside.

"Calm down," said Connie; "you're all excited. Bully for you, but calm down."

"Wait—wait a minute and I'll calm down. I—can't do it all of a sudden. Now—now I'm going to do something else—wait till I tell you——"

Connie put his arm over the quivering form of the little Elk mascot who seemed now to be launched upon a wild debauch of heroism. "Hsh, all right, Shorty. You did fine; gee, I have to laugh. The patrol won't believe you did it."

"Now you got to help me do something else," said Skinny, gulping with excitement and satisfaction.

"Surest thing."

"You got to—to-morrow morning early I'm

going to swim across the lake and get the Hiawatha Prize.''

"Goodness me!"

"Yop—I'm going to swim across and get it. So will you get all the patrol up early so some of you can row across while I swim?"

"Listen, Shorty," said Connie. "You did one peach of a stunt; the patrol will go crazy when they hear it. Why Hunt Ward tried for that; you remember. The Silver Foxes tried for it—Roy Blakeley. That was the time he didn't do all the laughing."

"And maybe now they won't make fun of me, hey?"

"Listen, Shorty; go in and go to sleep now. And don't be thinking you can do everything just because you did this."

"I'm going to, I'm going to——"

"No you're not. You're not going to try for the Hiawatha canoe, because that isn't in your line. See? You little sneaky devil, you! Went in your bare feet, huh? Go on in and go to bed now and don't talk ragtime. What's the matter, aren't you satisfied?"

"I got to go——"

"Yes, you *got to go*—to bed. To-morrow we'll go over to Administration Shack and have them take your picture. You can put on your new togs, dress up in your regular scout suit, all dolled up like a Christmas tree. You know they want pictures for *Boys' Life*, fellows that win awards and do stunts and all that. You go to bed now and when you get up in the morning put on your new scout duds. What the dickens are you afraid of? Nobody's going to kid you. And we'll go over and let Mr. Wainwright take a snapshot of you holding the pennant. *Alfred McCord of the Elk Patrol, Bridgeboro, New Jersey, holding the white pennant taken from a cabin where it was supposed to be guarded at Temple Camp, New York.* How does that sound? Go on in now, and remember when you get up in the morning put on your scout suit. That's your patrol leader's order. You're all right, Shorty, you're a little winner!''

So this was the sequel of his triumph. *"Put on your scout suit."* A fine mess he had made of it. He knew Connie Bennett for a sober, sensible boy, who more than most patrol leaders had some notion of leadership and discipline. So Connie had known about the scout suit and had just not pushed him in the matter of wearing it. But now there was to be no more nonsense. Here was the penalty of heroism. What was he to do? It was clear from the way

Connie spoke that the try for the Hiawatha Prize was quite out of the question; they did not regard him as a swimmer. What he would be expected to do, would be compelled to do, was put on his new scout suit and go to Administration Shack with his patrol and have his picture taken as the capturer of the white pennant. And all his fine plan of helping Danny to get out from the shadow of fearful peril would go for naught. This was Skinny's first experience in being a "really truly" hero.

There was a vein of something running in the McCord family. I don't know whether you would call it a vein of the heroic or just a vein of recklessness and rebelliousness. Diffident and sensitive little Skinny had a touch of it. Perhaps it was this that bound him to Danny. At all events there was this about him. His temperament was one of sweet diffidence, of a smiling shyness which made him a subject both for banter and affection. At the other extreme in his strange make-up was the capacity for utter frenzy. I suppose you might say that he was highly strung and afraid to show it until something tipped the scales of his delicate nature. There was no such thing as authority then.

They would not take this capturer of the

white pennant seriously. Well then, he did not care. There was only one person in the world who could have dominated him then, and that was Danny. But it was for Danny that he was now possessed by a will so strong that it made his poor little body tremble. Danny could not help him; he was going to help Danny. He was possessed, inspired, this little fellow who smiled quaintly when they made fun of him. He did not sleep that night; he lay trembling with a towering resolve.

Early in the morning, while still his comrades were sleeping, he crept out of bed, pulled on the only clothes he had and started out. The grass was all covered with sparkling dew; the air was crisp and clear, the birds were making a great chorus in the trees as if they had over-slept and were in a hurry. Skinny had a queer little trot, something between a walk and run, that boys took delight in imitating. He did not look in the least like the scout on the cover of the Handbook. .

He went down the hill on which the memorial cabins stood, casting a glance up through the woods to the point where the little shanty was. So clear was the morning that he might even have glimpsed it through the trees, only it was in the overgrown cut and below the line

of vision. He wondered what sort of a night
Danny had spent. The thought recurred to
him (it had recurred many times in that event-
ful, sleepless night) that maybe bloodhounds
had found him—found his half-brother who had
knocked Kinney senseless—and had barked
their beastly exultation to human pursuers.
But that could not be; Blythedale Reform
School was too far way for that sort of pursuit. Nevertheless Skinny's blood tingled at
the thought.

He was barefoot, for the business he was on
required no shoes. He trotted down around
the main pavilion, cut through the big open
"grub" shed and pattered along the board walk
to Administration Shack. This was the holy-
of-holies of Temple Camp, sanctum of officials,
where there was a safe and a counter and a
young man forever playing away at a typewriter machine. Skinny had never before ventured upon the veranda of this official lair, and
he trod with reverence. Above the bulletin
board near the door was a framed set of rules
for the information of guests. Skinny wanted
to confirm his knowledge by one of these and
he read it with delight:

> XI The office will be open for the
> transaction of general business

from 10 to 11 o'clock A.M. and
from 2 to 3 o'clock P.M.

So Danny could not enroll as Danville Bently until ten o'clock. He hoped that Danny had not yet destroyed the letter and that it might still reach the office. He went around to the side of the building and tried to look through the window, but it was too high. So he dragged a bench over from the "grub" shed and stood on that.

Within was a large glass case filled with forest trophies. And there in a corner (he had seen it before) stood the Hiawatha Prize canoe. He just wanted to make sure that it was there. Down he jumped and off he ran toward the float where the boats were knocking and clanking their chains. The water was rough and looked cold. He pulled off his faded shirt and shabby trousers and walked out to the end of the springboard. Even his light weight caused its metal parts to squeak; it always squeaked in the morning owing to the dampness of the night and the few hours of disuse. For just a moment he paused, then plunged into the lake.

CHAPTER X

WON

Over near the opposite shore of the lake there was a man fishing from a boat that morning. He sat motionless in the early solitude, a lonely figure against the somber background of wooded shore. Across the lake was a ribbon of light, like a silvery stream flowing in the dark water. It seemed to scatter into bits of tinsel where it touched the base of the densely covered heights. The lone fisherman was not in its path.

Suddenly he raised his rod, swinging the long line far off from the opposite side of his boat, and just then something caught his eye. About fifty yards distant an object was moving across the shimmering band. At first he thought it was a freakish manifestation of this glimmering sheen. Then he saw that it was a foreign object, progressing slowly, steadily. It reached the clearly defined border of this shining area; then he lost it for a few moments.

Now it appeared again coming straight toward him; by-times he caught a glimpse of a face; an arm appeared and disappeared regularly. On, on the swimmer came with slow, unswerving progress. The fisherman heard a distant bell; like an answering peal it echoed from the solemn heights near by. Distant voices could be heard, thin and spent. The man could not hear what they said as they seemed to dissolve in the air. But the bell continued ringing. He felt rather than heard distant excitement. The ringing and the voices were mellowed by the intervening space, yet he sensed that something was wrong over at the big camp.

The swimmer was now in plain view of the fisherman—close at hand. He did not seem to be in trouble, but a swim across Black Lake was by no means an easy feat, and the man hauled in his line and sculled over to intercept him.

"Don't touch me—keep away!" Skinny fairly yelled.

"Don't you want to come aboard?"

"No, you keep away from me!"

The boy seemed in a frenzy; it was evident that he was nearly exhausted with only his will power to keep him going. The man, apprehensive of disaster, sculled alongside him. Soon the little fellow's feet were on the bottom and as he staggered through the shallow water it was evident that he was at the point of collapse. *"Keep away, don't touch me!"* he kept saying. Then he groped blindly for the branch of a projecting tree, and so guided his tottering way to the steep bank, where he sank down unconscious. He could not quiver in every nerve as he did in his former triumph, for oblivion came and he knew not that he, Skinny McCord, had won the Hiawatha prize canoe!

The fisherman did not know that this drenched and ghostly pale boy had done anything more than a rash stunt. He lifted him gently and laid him in the boat and started to row across toward camp. But he did not have to go far. Across the lake at top speed the camp launch came chugging, filled with eager, shouting passengers.

"Is he all right?" a voice called. "Isn't drowned, is he?"

"No, but he's fainted," the man called back.

"Did you pick him up?"

"No, he made the shore."

Up she came to the old flat-bottomed boat that rocked in the swell as Councilor Wallace caught hold of the unpainted rail while two scouts lifted Skinny into the launch. All the Elks were there, and Doc Carson, first aid scout of the Ravens, and Tom Slade, the young camp

assistant. Yes, the little devil was all right.
He opened his eyes and closed them again.
Connie Bennett, his patrol leader, brushed the
soaked hair away from the small white forehead, and the eyes opened again and the quivering lips smiled at Connie. ''You're all right,
kid?'' said he gently. He pulled away a bit of
water-weed that was plastered across the little
fellow's face. ''Want to try to sit up?''

''I see him a comin','' said the fisherman,
''an' I kinder surmised somethin's wrong. He
wuz swimmin' all ragged—I never see nuthin'
like it. But he yells to me not ter touch 'im.
Just screeches at me. Then he goes reelin' up
the shore 'n' grabs hold on a tree 'n' goes
twistin' roun' 'n' down he goes. Maybe he wuz
escapin' thinks I.''

''No, he wasn't escaping,'' said Connie. ''He
just had a kind of a craze on. He did a stunt
and he thought he'd like to try a still bigger
one.''

''He's a lucky kid,'' said the fisherman as he
rowed away.

''Lucky patrol,'' said one of the boys.

They took him over to camp and into Administration Shack and laid him on the couch there.
And in a little while he was quite restored and
able to go up the hill to his patrol cabin. His

slim little form looked funny in a bathrobe as he trudged along, tripping now and again. The Elks clustered all about him proudly. Stut Moran playfully pulled the tasseled cord tight about him and tied it in a knot; it made him look still funnier, and he smiled that bashful smile of his to see them amused at his expense. "Looks like a champion prize-fighter on his way to the ring," said Stut.

"Well you've got a nice new dry suit anyway," said Connie. "And you're going to put it on and have your picture taken for both things that you did. Jumping jiminies, kid, you sure did break loose! What are you going to do next? Why, you crazy little midnight sneak! How the dickens did you suppose you were going to prove you swam across the lake when you got up at about fourteen-twenty A.M. and started off without any escort. Suppose that man hadn't been there. It's all right, kid, we're not kicking; we've got the Hiawatha canoe, gee we've got no kick, I'll say that. But cut out the hero stuff for a couple of days. Why, you skinny little grasshopper, you've been running wild!"

"Can I get it right away?" Skinny asked. "The canoe, can I get it right away quick? Right away *now*, can I get it?" he persisted, tripping over the bathrobe which was as much too big for him as his lost scout suit. "Can I honest and true get it right away *now?*"

"Who's going to stop us?" laughed Connie.

"We'll be out paddling in it this afternoon," said Vic Norris.

"Do you know what I was thinking?" Bert McAlpin asked.

"Skinny doesn't think, he acts," said Connie.

"No, but on the level," said Bert. "I never took such an awful lot of interest in it before— I mean the regatta—but, *jiminies,* as long as we've got the Hiawatha canoe why can't a couple of us train up and go in for the Mary Temple Cup? Skinny's too small, but it's all in the patrol anyway. You know what Roy Blakeley's all the time saying—united we stand, divided we sprawl. I say let's a couple of us train for the canoe races. Skinny's got us started now and we'll do big things. *Oh boy,* the white pennant! And now the canoe. Oh boy, Skinny's the big noise in camp."

He did not make much noise as he sat down on the edge of his cot, his clamorous comrades all about him. He had never tasted glory before. He had not only made a sensational hop, skip and jump into fame; he had aroused in his patrol the thirst for still greater achievement. He was bewildered, frightened.

"Listen here, kid," said Connie, "I'm so blamed excited I can hardly talk straight. Listen here. The breakfast horn will be sounding in a few minutes. We're not washed up yet, we got called up in such a hurry. While we're getting ready for breakfast you get on your new scout suit and we'll meet you over at 'eats.' Now no more blamed nonsense, you do what I tell you and put on your scout suit, and come over to 'eats' all dolled up right so the bunch will know the fellow that did these things is a scout. Understand?"

Skinny understood, and he just sat on the edge of his cot, nervous and anxious to be left alone. To these enthusiastic, planning comrades, his achievement was a climax. But it was no climax to him; it was just one step in what he intended to do. He was bewildered and nervous at their talk about future triumphs with the prize canoe. Connie's order to him about the new scout suit troubled him. You see, Skinny had not intended to be a hero. He was a hero worshipper, and his hero was Danny. He had never thought to complicate matters by being a hero himself. Now he saw that being a hero was a nuisance.

CHAPTER XI

IF

Skinny knew that Danny was wise, that he would not appear in camp before half past nine, because there was no boat or train which would permit his arrival before that time. Danny's attention to detail in his free and lawless progress commanded admiration if not respect. He never committed a silly blunder. Also Skinny knew that this runaway brother of his could not commit the perilous act of false registration until the office opened at ten o'clock. So there was time enough for what he had planned to do.

Hurriedly opening his old suit-case, he pulled out the only extra shirt and trousers that he had and put them on. Then he locked the suit-case again so that no prying comrade might discover that the new suit was not there. Just as he started from the cabin the breakfast horn sounded. He hurried along with that funny shuffling sideways gait of his and paused at the cooking shack to get an apple and a sandwich from Chocolate Drop, the colored chef. Any

scout contemplating a short hike was welcome
to this customary refreshment. He wanted it
for Danny. He wondered how Danny had spent
the night and hoped he had not been aroused
by all the fuss caused by his early swim. At
cooking shack he took occasion to ask Chocolate Drop if he knew where Helmer Clarkson
stayed.

"He dat boy wots folks done send 'im big
grapefruit 'n' boxes wi' dem figs. Sho he done
sleep up dere yonder in one dem woods cabins.
You know dat cabin wi' de skunk skin tacked
on de do'? Lor' Massa Skincord, dat boy am
rich! Him folk send him *great big* crate full
of fruit. Dat ain't good fer no young boy, dat
ain't. Bein' diffrent, *dat am bad*. I say ter
Massa Slade, I say, dat ain't no camp scout
business. Share one, share all, in dis yer camp,
dat's wot I say. You gwine straight up dat
path, you'll find it."

It was little enough that poor Skinny knew
about the unwise procedure of rich parents
with their sons at camp. I dare say Chocolate
Drop was right; there was too much pampering.
Certainly no one had ever sent Skinny a grapefruit or a box of figs. Something in the little
fellow's wistful look touched the kindly heart
of Chocolate Drop, who reigned unquestioned

monarch in the fragrant cook shack, and he made up an extra sandwich and handed it to him together with four cookies. "You watch out you don' get bit by dem rattlesnakes," he warned. Rattlesnakes were the terror of Chocolate Drop's life. "You jes' good as dat Clarkson son. Now you scamper off ter breakfast."

But Skinny did not go to breakfast. He started up the hill, encouraged, elated. He was going to do business with a boy who had expressed a desire for a canoe, and whose people were so rich that they sent him figs and grapefruit. He did not know just exactly how he would approach such a boy; he dreaded this more than he had dreaded his swim across the lake. But, of course, rich boys could be talked to.

He was not exactly afraid; he felt that luck had favored him thus far. He had lifted the white pennant and had been able thereby to conceal the real purpose of his absence at night. He had won the Hiawatha canoe. And now he was going to sell it to a boy who was so rich that he received delicacies by parcel post. That would be easy. Then he would hurry on up to the old shanty in the cut and give Danny the food and the money. After that he would, of course, worry about Danny's escape from the reform school. But at least the dangers at Temple Camp would be averted.

On arriving at the cabin with the skunk skin tacked on the door, Skinny was astonished to find that it was the very cabin from which he had taken the white pennant. The place looked different in the daylight. He had not seen the skunk skin on his nocturnal raid, nor the quaintly worded sign above the door which read:

THE ALLIGATORS OF ALLEGHANY

But he saw clearly the hole from which he had so stealthily lifted the pennant staff. The Alligators had not gone down to breakfast; there were voices inside. He wondered whether his little masterstroke would leave them prejudiced against him. Hardly that, he realized, for scouts are good sports and cheerful losers. Perhaps they would even give him credit, as the saying is. He was not doubtful about scouts, but he was a little afraid of a rich boy.

The voices inside were loud and angry; the occupants of the cabin seemed all talking at once and excitedly.

"Awh, forget it, and come ahead down to eats, will you?"

"I'm through," said another boy.

"If you're talking of breakfast I haven't even started yet," said still another. "For the love of Mike, will you cut it out and come on down."

"I'm through," said the boy who had made this pronouncement before.

"All right, we're satisfied," another said.

"Do you take back what you said?"

"No, I don't take back what I said."

There was a pause and Skinny tremblingly knocked on the door. It was opened by a tall scout whom he had seen before.

"Does Helmer Clarkson live here?" he asked, his voice shaking a little. He had quickly decided that he would not mention the affair of the white pennant.

"Sure, you're welcome to him," said a boy from within. "We give six coupons free to anybody who'll take him."

"Cut that out," said another boy.

"Here, put him in your pocket and take him home," said still another as he pushed a rather small boy through the open door. It was evident that the victim of this hearty eviction was the Rockefeller of Temple Camp, Helmer Clarkson. He was an effeminate looking boy; rather sissified, Skinny thought. It was easy to be-

lieve that he was of a sort to be the recipient
of dainties from home.

Skinny, in his simplicity, went straight to the
point. "Do you want to buy a canoe?" he
asked.

"What canoe?" asked a boy from inside.

"The Hiawatha Prize canoe," said Skinny,
addressing Clarkson, as they all gathered about
the doorway staring and listening. "I heard
you wanted to buy a canoe and I'll sell you that
one for as much—I mean—only fifteen dollars."
He was too simple to place the price at a little
more than Danny needed. The canoe was actually worth seventy dollars.

"What's the big idea?" somebody asked.

"*You!*" laughed another. "What are *you*
doing with the prize canoe? You mean that
one in the headquarters building?"

"I won it by swimming across the lake," said
Skinny, blushing to the roots of his hair, "and
I don't want it because—because it's my own
business why I don't want it. So do you want
to buy it for fifteen dollars? I heard you
wanted one."

"I'm leaving this camp and I don't want it,"
said Helmer Clarkson.

"He hasn't got the price," a boy taunted.

For answer Helmer Clarkson displayed the

contents of a neat wallet which almost staggered poor Skinny. "I've had enough of this
camp," he said, "and I'm going home on the
noon train from Catskill."

"It's only fifteen dollars," poor Skinny said.
"Maybe I'd take ten."

"If you gave me the canoe for nothing I
wouldn't stay here," said Helmer Clarkson in
a very mincing manner. "If you'd come
around two or three days ago—even yesterday
—I might have given you twenty-five dollars for
it. I can spend fifty dollars for one if I want
to. But I've had enough of this crowd, thank
you. I'm going home."

Poor Skinny's hopes were dashed. He cast
a forlorn look at the scouts, who were laughing
heartily. They were not laughing at him; for
once he was not the victim. They were laughing (and that with a kind of tolerant contempt)
at Helmer Clarkson.

"Yes, we got no canoes to-day," one boy
sang.

"I don't want to play in your yard," sang
another.

"Tell him why you're going home, Ellie,"
a third shouted.

"I'll tell him," another volunteered. "You
know we had the white pennant up here—we

took it away from that Virginia troop over near
Turtle Cove. Each one of us is supposed to
stay awake forty minutes every night and listen. Last night our little sleeping beauty—
that's him—falls asleep at the switch. Somebody walked away with the pennant. We even
knew somebody was hanging around, because
just a little while before that I sneaked out and
caught a fellow nosing about. On top of that
Sweet-dream Ellie has to go to sleep when his
turn was on. And—listen, get this—when we
jump very gently on his neck he gets sore and
says he won't play any more."

During the recital of this indictment, Helmer
Clarkson held himself aloof in silent dignity.
"I'm through with the scouts for good," said
he. "It was only an experiment anyway. But
I certainly do love canoing——"

"Sure, in the bathtub," interrupted one of
the boys.

"*Chief Dead-to-the-world* sailing down the
Alleghany River," mocked another.

"If it wasn't for my leaving," said Helmer,
ignoring them, "I'd be only too glad to buy
your canoe. I'd have given you more than
fifteen dollars for it."

Skinny looked from one to the other of this
cheery group; they seemed an interesting pa-

trol, notwithstanding their family disturbance.
Then his eyes fell on Helmer Clarkson in a
woebegone, incredulous gaze. He realized that
by his own act of "lifting" the pennant he had
effectually prevented the sale of the canoe. If
he had not stolen up in the dead of night,
so softly that the dozing Helmer never heard
him, he might now have fifteen dollars—thirty
perhaps—with which to speed his erring brother
forth to safety.

What a tragic word is IF!

CHAPTER XII

SCOUT LAW NUMBER TWO

He had taken the white pennant. He had won the Hiawatha Prize. He had brought glory to his patrol. But all he had to give Danny was two sandwiches and four cookies. Hero though he was, he could not face his colleagues, for he had no scout suit to put on. So long as there was hope of selling the canoe, he had not considered what his patrol would think of this. He had thought only of Danny. But now, as he trudged on up through the woods, a forlorn little fellow, he wondered what Connie and the others would say when they heard that he had tried to sell the prize canoe. They would certainly hear that, and he could not tell them why he had attempted such an unscoutlike business. There was never any buying and selling of prizes at Temple Camp.

He trudged up through the woods, cautiously looking back now and then. It seemed to him a very long time since he had seen Danny, so much had happened in the meantime. He found him sitting on the shelf in the shanty, his knees

75

drawn up to form a reading desk on which the Scout Handbook lay open.

"Hey, Tiny, this is some book," said he. "Honest, do they do all these things, or is it just bunk? Here's a good one on page—page— here it is, sixty-six. This is the one for me. Here's a gold medal you get for saving a guy's life, only you've got to risk your own. If you lose your life you're out of luck. If you get away with it they hand you this——"

"I know all about it," said Skinny.

"That ain't so worse," said Danny, idly running over the pages. "Wait till I find—oh here it is, here's a pippin! Here's where a guy makes out he's a smuggler—page four hundred and thirty—and the bunch has to track him. If he gets to the nearest town he's K.O. I ought to be able to get away with that, Tiny." It was certainly in his line. "They got some good dope here, all right," he added. "You can even be one if you're not in with a bunch."

"That's a pioneer scout," said Skinny.

"Here's a nifty—listen to this one. They got a lot of badges you can win. Here's one on riding a horse——"

"I know all about them," Skinny repeated.

It was evident that scouts had merits which

Danny could admire, but had no desire to imi-
tate. His rather nonchalant attitude toward
scouting troubled poor Skinny. He had spent
the whole night in nervous tension, planning
and striving to save Danny from his own folly.
And here was Danny leisurely inspecting the
Scout Handbook, commenting upon its features
with eminent fairness, and apparently without
a care in the world. It must be admitted that
so far as looks were concerned there was not a
boy at Temple Camp more scoutlike than he.
Poor Skinny's suit fitted him to perfection; it
was in line with this blithesome young scape-
grace's luck that his ungainly little half-brother
had in his innocence bought the suit too large.
Though, indeed, poor Skinny would never in
any suit look as natty as this self-sufficient
brother of his. The only false note in Danny's
ensemble was a rakish tilt of the scout hat,
which gave him a rather too easy-going and
sophisticated air.

"I brought you something to eat," said poor
Skinny. "I was afraid they'd find you, those
reform school people, but I'm glad they didn't.
There's two sandwiches here, and four cookies.
I bet you didn't sleep much—I bet."

"You lose your bet," said Danny. "I was
dead to the cruel world. Some blamed bird or

other, that was screaming like Hail Columbia,
woke me up.''

"Those are blue jays," said Skinny.

"They'd be black and blue jays if I caught
them," said Danny. "I went over there to a
spring and washed up. Then I came back and
started giving this book the once-over. What
time is it anyway? Can I go and do my act
yet?" He ate the sandwiches while Skinny
talked.

"I tried to get fifteen dollars for you so you
wouldn't have to stay here and I swam across
the lake so as to win the prize canoe; I did it
early this morning, Danny, and I won it. But
the feller I tried to sell it to because he's rich
and has grapefruit sent him and everything—
that feller wouldn't buy it, because he's mad at
his patrol and he's going home, because they're
sore at him on account of his not staying awake
so nobody could take the pennant. I'm the one
that took it. So I'm the one to blame, because
I can't give you fifteen dollars."

Danny was a boy who was always ready to
do anything. Consequently nothing that any
other boy did astonished him. He was interested in propositions to do things. He was not
so interested in things that had been done. So
all he said was, "You should worry."

"I *got* to worry," said poor Skinny.

"And I've got to stay here and I might as well have some fun," said Danny.

Poor Skinny was aghast at Danny's utter inability to perceive the peril in which he stood. This impersonation of another boy at Temple Camp was to be merely another casual adventure in the blithesome career of Danny. He had lost no sleep over it, he apprehended no complications. He would cross bridges when he came to them. He was not annoyed by Skinny's near success in the matter of the canoe. What Skinny had done did not seem to impress him as an exploit. Since he was not able to supply fifteen dollars, Danny accepted scouting as a means of escape. And he was not going to worry about it.

"Will you promise—cross your heart—that you won't say I told you to do it?" Skinny asked, with panic fear in every feature. "Will you promise—honest and true, cross your heart —that you won't ever even *look* at me?"

"Go on down and get your breakfast, kid," said Danny.

"I tried to get you the money so you could go away."

"Sure, you should worry; go down and eat, Tiny."

"And you won't go to the office till about half past ten, because on account of the train?"

"Leave it to me, kid."

"You're going to get in a lot of trouble," Skinny warned, pathetically apprehensive.

Poor little fellow, he had done the best he could to avert this bizarre and perilous undertaking of Danny's. He had risked his life. He was doomed to trouble with his comrades because of the missing scout suit, and because of his attempt to sell the reward of his heroism. They would not even laugh at him and make fun of him any more. He wondered if he had better go ask the Alligators of Alleghany not to mention the offer he had made at their cabin. But that would only discredit him with them; it would look sneaky.

Such troubles to arise from good intentions and deeds of skill and prowess! Poor Skinny, his excursion into the field of heroism had not been propitious. And pressing down upon him more heavily than all these perplexities was the terrifying thought of Danny. What might happen there made Skinny shudder. Such an act of effrontery as his half-brother was launched upon quite unnerved this poor little scout who had been so humble and obscure. Yet he was staunch in loyalty to Danny. He would bear the scornful taunts (as he had always borne the humorous taunts) of Temple Camp if that were necessary. And when the worst came to the worst he would be loyal to Danny. It was odd that through all this disheartening mess, he did not once recall with pride and elation that he was the winner of the Hiawatha Prize. He had forgotten all about the canoe.

CHAPTER XIII

ALIAS DANVILLE BENTLY

He hurried along with his queer, shuffling gait to the big shed where meals were served in pleasant weather. He was always insignificant looking unless you looked straight into his eyes. There was something indescribable about those eyes that haunted one. They bespoke a latent frenzy that could carry that homely little frail body to any heights of heroism. But all you saw as he hurried along was a little codger who somehow reminded you of the slums. He had the scared look so familiar in homeless dogs.

As he moved between the long tables a few scouts who had never noticed him before, turned and stared at him. "Honest?" one scout asked his neighbor. "Sure, that's him," said another; "that's the one." By no means all of them knew of his triumphant swim. At one table they were talking about the "lifting" of the white pennant, but no one seemed to know that he was the hero of that affair. One would have to be a pretty big hero to divert the attention of the Temple Camp scouts while they were eating breakfast. One remark he did overhear as he made his way to the tables of his own troop. "Special bargain sale in prize canoes," he heard a boy say. "Business is not so good today," another boy answered. Skinny flushed but did not glance at the authors of this cheap sarcasm.

The Bridgeboro Troop occupied two tables, the Ravens and the Chipmunks at one, the Silver Foxes and the Elks at the other. As Skinny edged into his seat only one voice greeted him. The exuberant Roy Blakeley of the Silver Foxes called. "Hey Skinny, you were in the swim all right, but not here.

> Sticks and stones can break your bones,
> But looks can never hurt you."

But there Roy Blakeley was mistaken. Looks did hurt Skinny; they were like blows to his sensitive nature. And now nothing but black looks greeted him. Something was wrong evidently; something very serious. For there was no criticism, no half-humorous slurs and sallies. The members of his patrol passed him things at the table, and once or twice asked such service from him, and it was pitiful to see him respond with such alacrity. But no one talked with him—with this boy who had "lifted" the white pennant and won the Hiawatha canoe. He thought it must be because he had not donned his scout suit.

After breakfast he went off by himself and wandered up into the woods. He often did that to get away from the bantering scouts, but this morning he was beset with forebodings. Something was wrong, everything was wrong. The atmosphere he had felt at breakfast pervaded the whole quiet woodland. Something played on the strings of his delicate nature, causing them to vibrate with strange apprehension. He felt nervous, ill at ease; he knew something was going to happen. Up in the woods was an oriole's nest which he had been watching, for he intended to take it when it was deserted and claim the Audubon Prize. He sat down on a stump and looked at it now, hanging up in the tree like a dried rag. He had no more interest in the prizes. He had won the hardest one of all to win, and it had brought him nothing but trouble.

After a little while, he wandered back to camp again, haunted by that strange sense of foreboding. A lonesome, forlorn little waif he seemed; hopelessly an odd number; not one single sign of the scout about him. Just a little

codger from Corkscrew Alley. Passing a few
yards from Administration Shack he saw the
usual coming and going by which he knew that
the office was open. There were the usual
loiterers on the porch, scoutmasters hurrying in
and out, new boys glancing around as they
emerged and pausing to read the notices.

Suddenly a rather tall boy with his scout hat
tilted at a rakish angle came out, folding a
paper. That was the set of rules that they gave
to every new arrival. He also held a red card
and Skinny knew what that meant. It meant
he was registered as a scout without troop af-
filiation and was assigned to the big dormitory
which, with several group cabins, formed what
was called Pioneer Row.* So Danny had come
through the routine of enrollment without
trouble. Skinny was even proud of him, he
looked so natty, so self-assured, so different
from those bewildered looking new arrivals who
glanced bashfully about seeming not to know
what to do with themselves. There was one
whole patrol of them and they seemed as help-
less as a pack of sheep.

As Danny stepped down off the porch he
passed between two scouts who were catching

* A pioneer scout is one without a troop or patrol. See
page 24 of the Scout Handbook.

ball and he raised his arm in an offhand way intercepting the ball and throwing it to a third boy. How proud Skinny would have been of this charmingly nonchalant brother, except for that frightful secret! Even as it was he felt relieved and a little proud, Danny was so attractive and seemed so safe—so equal to any emergency.

Skinny hardly knew where to go so he went down to the springboard. Still that vague feeling of presentiment beset him and made him nervous. Sitting on the springboard were Connie Bennett, his patrol leader, and several of the Elk Patrol. Seeing Skinny approaching, Stut Moran and Vic Norris strolled away. "Cut that out," Connie said to them, but they paid no attention.

Skinny could not bear the tension; his little frame was trembling with nervous excitement. "What's the matter?" he forced himself to ask. "If I don't want to wear my—a—scout suit I don't have to, do I? If I don't want to have my picture taken in it, I don't have to."

Hearing him speak, Stut and Vic turned and paused, Vic calling, "Come on, you scouts, let him alone. Don't you know what we said?"

The others started from the springboard to join Stut and Vic. Skinny remained on the springboard, scarlet with embarrassment. Like a little statue of lonely poverty he stood there on the board from which he had plunged for his sensational swim.

"Can't you tell me if it's about the suit?" he called almost imploringly.

They seemed to be conferring and he waited. Then Connie beckoned and he went to them, like a dog doubtful of its welcome. Thus it happened that one of the most memorable events of Temple Camp occurred on the grassy patch near the shore, just under the big willow tree where they painted the boats before launching them. Scouts will show you the spot now.

"I'm going to give you the chance to deny it, that's only fair," Connie said. "Did you try to sell the Hiawatha Prize to a patrol from out in Pennsylvania?"

"Yes, I did," Skinny said. He was trembling, not in fear, but in the pride of his frankness.

"You did!"

"Yes, I did—I said I did."

There was a tense pause.

"A *prize!* You tried to sell it for money," exclaimed Vic Norris incredulously.

"Didn't you know those scouts are going in

for the canoe races the same as we are?"

"No, I didn't know that," Skinny protested, breathing heavily.

Such an altercation could not fail to attract lookers-on and perhaps a dozen boys were now standing about listening.

"Well, you knew *we* were going in the races with it," Connie said. "And you knew that prizes kind of go to patrols. You ask anybody in Temple Camp — ask Tom Slade — if he ever *heard* of a scout trying to *sell* a camp award. Jiminies, I didn't believe it when I heard it. You sneaked up to those fellows' cabin and asked them if they wanted to buy the Hiawatha canoe for fifteen dollars. Did you or didn't you?"

"If you can prove you didn't, we won't chuck you out," Bert McAlpin said.

"I said I did," said Skinny, standing his ground, but with a tremor in his voice, "but I didn't sneak."

"Good night!" groaned Hunt Ward disgustedly.

"What did you want to do it for?" Connie asked. He alone seemed disposed to be considerate.

"Because—it's none of anybody's business what I did it for," Skinny said.

"Why it's like the gold medal; would you sell that?"

"Yes, I would if I thought—if I was sure it was right to do it," Skinny said.

Perhaps some of the onlookers sympathized with him, he was so small, so insignificant looking; and withal so eager and earnest. Tears were rolling down his cheeks now and he raised his shabby little sleeve to wipe his eyes and still stood his ground in trembling defiance. "I would and it's none of nobody's business," he said.

"*Oh, is that so?*" sneered Stut Moran. "If you wanted money as bad as all that why couldn't you steal it like you did apples from Schmitter's Grocery when you'd have got in trouble if Mr. Ellsworth hadn't taken you into the troop?"

Skinny trembled, but said nothing. "Did I —I—did I act all right since I was in the troop?" he finally managed to get out.

"Sure, trying to sell prizes," Vic Norris shot at him angrily. "Gee we've had enough of Corkscrew Alley in our troop. You don't belong in the troop anyway, you dirty little slum rat, you——"

There was a slight stir in the group and there in front of Victor Norris stood a boy he had never seen before, a boy whose scout hat was tilted at a rakish angle and whose half-closed eyes were like cold steel.

"Do you take that back?" said he.

"You mind your own business; I take nothing back," said Vic.

The blow fell so swiftly that he was sprawling on the ground before the onlookers knew what had happened. They will tell you now at Temple Camp that that blow sounded as if it fell on a wooden surface, so terrific was the force of it. The dazed victim rubbed his eye half-consciously and made as if to rise. Like lightning his assailant brushed aside an interfering spectator and looked behind him to see if any official might be approaching. "Don't get up till you take it back," he said in quick, businesslike fashion. "You'll just go down again. Keep away, you fellers. Well?"

"I take it back," cried Vic Norris.

"Tell him, don't tell me," said the strange boy, indicating Skinny.

And he strolled away as if the matter no further concerned him.

CHAPTER XIV

THE PIONEER SCOUT

But it was not Vic Norris who was hurt; it was Skinny. He would not, he could not, tell them the truth. He must live in the shadow of their cruel thoughts. Mr. Ellsworth, scoutmaster of the troop, arrived in camp on Friday for the week end, and tried to smooth over the difficulty. But Skinny would not tell him why he had made his astonishing offer to the departed Helmer Clarkson. Nor would he say why he would not wear his scout suit. He was as stubborn as a little mule in those matters. Mr. Ellsworth told the Elks that they would just have to take Skinny as they found him, that there was no explaining him. He reminded them that at all events they had the canoe, and the white pennant.

So they took Skinny as they found him, and they found him different. He seemed worried and preoccupied, and took little interest in the patrol. They never asked him to wear his scout suit and he continued to be, what he had always been in camp, an odd little figure in a faded

blouse. Those in the Bridgeboro troop who
were most discerning noticed how he seemed
always in fear. But when they made fun of
him, as they were wont to do at camp-fire, he
smiled bashfully in the same old way and was
delightfully ill at ease.

He occasionally went out in the prize canoe
with scouts of his patrol and sat wedged into
one end like a funny little figurehead. You
would never have dreamed that he was the
boy who had won that trim craft which
skimmed so lightly in the water. But he seemed
to appreciate being taken out in it. Perhaps
after all it was not Skinny who had won the
canoe. It was the frenzied and despairing soul
of Skinny which had done that. Anyway, they
often took him out in it and he sat very still
and upright as he was told to do.

The Elks soon lost the white pennant; a scout
in a Vermont troop walked away with it one
night during Vic Norris' watch, so Vic had two
black eyes in a way of speaking. Bert McAlpin
tried to get it back and was caught red-handed.
Then Connie himself tried and got a good laugh
from the Vermonters. Skinny was not particularly interested in these attempts; he was too
much worried about Danny to concern himself
with patrol exploits. He saw Danny every day

and occasionally spoke with him, but they were not much together. The terrible thing that Danny was doing made Skinny afraid of him; he stood in awe of such daring and effrontery.

As for Danny, he was not in the least troubled. On the very day of his arrival he hiked to Catskill, keeping off the highway, and sent a telegram collect, in the name of Temple Camp, advising the father of Danville Bently that his son would be expected on August Second. Having come safely through the formality of enrollment, no embarrassing questions were asked him and indeed he had no further intercourse with the management. Temple Camp is a big place and he was soon absorbed in its life. Nobody cared where he lived or anything else about him; they were all too busy with scouting.

And he was busy with scouting too. He might have taken his second class tests, he might even have qualified for the first class, but he cautiously refrained from any step which might bring him face to face with trustees and councilors. Since he did not seek the first class ranking he could not try for merit badges. He became, in short, one of those nondescript scouts who are to be found in every summer camp, boys who have taken the scout

oath and put on scout suits and let it go at that.
He was too large to be thought of as a tenderfoot; moreover his prowess and skill lifted him
out of that class. He was good at everything,
but he did not fit his exploits into the scout
program.

He bunked in Pioneer Row with that miscel-
laneous company whose members had come to
Temple Camp without troop or patrol. Many
of them were instances of the one lucky boy in
some homekeeping scout unit. Some of them
were active and clever, but they were deprived
of the advantages of group spirit. A boy scout
is better off with his patrol in a vacant lot than
alone at the best of scout camps. The big
sleeping quarters of Pioneer Row had more
the atmosphere of a boarding school dormitory
than of a scout camp. In a sense they did form
one big troop—too big.

After the first few days of his life in this
rather inglorious department of the spreading
community, Danny lost all fear of being found
out at camp. The whole thing had been so
easy! And Temple Camp was so embracing
and friendly! He was an adaptable boy and he
felt quite at home. He still feared the grim
authorities of the reform school, for he knew
that he had been committed to that hated insti-

tution by the State and that the long arm of the law was reaching out for him. But as the days passed and nothing happened, his fear subsided. He was so cozy and remote that discovery from either quarter seemed an altogether unlikely sequel of his good fortune. And August Second was so far away!

Once or twice he feared that Skinny might inadvertently, or in a spasm of outraged conscience, say something. But nothing happened and whatever fears he had were lulled to sleep. Yet there was one person there whom he should have feared and that was himself. But he not only did not fear himself; he did not fear anybody. The only trouble was that he would have to sneak away before August Second. Well, he thought, the authorities would have ceased their search for him by that time, and he would go away on a ship.

All the boys in Pioneer Dormitory liked Danny. He was more sophisticated than most of them and they stood somewhat in awe of him. He seemed to know a good deal about the world and they respected him for it. His rather nonchalant attitude toward scouting had something engaging in it; but there was one serious boy who was not too ready to fall under his spell.

This was Holman Sharpe, a pioneer scout from a farm in New Hampshire. He was not summering away from his troop; he had no troop. Nor was he, as so many of those boys were, the single remaining member of a disintegrated troop. He was a registered pioneer. In the lonely section where he lived there were no boys to form a troop. So he had sent to National Headquarters for blanks and had been enrolled as a pioneer scout, which was a very different thing from the unattached scouts of Pioneer Row.

This boy went in for scouting with both hands and feet and the easy-going Danny was greatly amused by him. He was one of those boys who take themselves very seriously. Such boys are found in schools and colleges, wrestling with their studies to the exclusion of everything else, forgetting life in the interest of learning. Scouting is not a good field in which to do this. There is nothing about scouting to study; it is just a form of life. But this boy conceived it as a sort of curriculum and the Handbook as a sort of text book. He was certainly born to be a student. It is not so certain that he was born to be a scout.

To this serious New England boy, Temple

Camp was a sort of university, the merit badges all representing study courses. He was out for promotion; he did not care so much about fun. His Handbook was all marked up with memorandums of his progress and notes of his plans. He was a canny boy and did not forget about the future. He even took into consideration the time when he would be too old for scouting and had his plans all made for joining the *Veteran Scout Association*. In an envelope he had three dollars laid away with which to buy the veteran pin several years hence.

Everything in the Handbook was law and gospel to him and he had set about the strenuous labor of squeezing it dry. He would get his money's worth at Temple Camp by doing every single thing that was even casually suggested in the scouting program. He had never had any give and take with other boys and he could not conceive of scouting being carried lightly and airily, as Roy Blakeley of the Silver Foxes, carried it. He *went in* for scouting with a vengeance.

What Danny did, he did easily, and he was highly entertained by the way Holman would come in carrying his Handbook and some maps and papers, and sit down on his cot, which was next to Danny's, to go over them and enter notes in his field book.

"Busy with your homework?" Danny would quiz.

"I've just hiked fourteen miles," Holman answered him one day. "I'm going to write it up to-night, and there's test four all finished on the first class badge. If you took all the miles you've used up flopping around in the woods to-day, I bet they'd run over fourteen and you'd have a seven mile double to lay up on your first class tests. I mixed some dough and cooked my dinner, too, while I was off, so I'm claiming the cooking badge on that. I don't know whether I'll get it or not."

"Did you ever study algebra?" Danny queried.

"Well, it's not exactly a part of scouting," said Holman.

Danny, sitting on Holman's cot with his knees drawn up, pulled his hat down over his forehead, which gave him a sophisticated, even a tough, look. "But I had the fun of flopping around in the woods," said he. "You hike so fast you never see anything."

"Make hay while the sun shines," said Holman in his businesslike way. "Why, you were telling me about following those marks and you came plunk on a rattlesnake; he's a pretty big one, I guess.''

"He was; he isn't any more," said Danny.

"You've got to look out how you kill those fellows. But what I was going to say was, you could use that stuff on the stalking test if you wanted to. Did you have any witnesses?''

"Only the rattlesnake and he's dead," said Danny.

"I'm only telling you how you waste your chances," said Holman. "You can do things, all right, only you don't think. I heard a scout over at the Kit Carson tents say you jumped over Outlet Brook.''

"Yere?''

"I've got it planned out so I can use one stunt on two tests.''

"Wholesale only, huh? What's that red book?'' Danny asked, kicking it.

"That? That's the English Handbook. I'll wager you that's the only one in camp. I guess you never even read the American one, do you?''

"Oh, I gave it the once over; there's some pretty good dope in it. Ever think you'd like to make a stab for the Gold Cross?''

"Life saving with imminent risk?'' (Holman quoted accurately). "That's something pretty high up; that's out of the ordinary."

"I was thinking I'd grab it—just for a
stunt," said Danny.

Holman shook his head, "That's one of the
big things—that's the very biggest," said he.
He knew all about it.

"That's the one for me," said Danny.

"I sort of don't like the way you refer to it."

"That's the snappiest one in the book," said
Danny.

"Talking about books," said Holman, "you
ought to look over this English Handbook; it's
by General Baden-Powell. There's a section in
it about deduction; deducing facts from clues
and signs. Why you can even look at a scout's
shoes and tell where he has been if you know
how."

"I don't care where's he's been," said
Danny.

"It's an interesting phase of scouting just
the same."

"Phase, huh? That's just detective stuff.
You don't want to be one of those guys, do
you?"

"Oh, that's part of scouting—mental effort."

"Yere?"

"Now, for instance, I've noticed something.
I even made a note of it."

"I bet you did."

"I don't believe there's a scout in this camp ever noticed that tattoo mark on your arm."

Danny started.

"Surprises you, eh?" Holman laughed. He did not often laugh. "Yes sir," he said in a way of small triumph, "I noticed it when you rolled up your sleeve; the time you reached down in the water after the compass that little big-eyed youngster is always losing. You rolled it away up—remember? I noticed. I said, 'That boy has known a sailor.' Now am I right?"

"Right—the first time."

"I wondered why the letters were D. M. since I knew your name was Danville Bently. But I hit on it. Now tell me if I'm right."

"Sure, you're always right."

"They name ships the *Molly B* and all like that. If a ship is called after a woman named Molly B. Smith, they just call it the *Molly B* I'll wager that M is your middle initial—Danville M. as you might say."

"*Geeee,* that's wonderful!" said Danny. "That's *simp*-ly wonderful! I bet you're going to keep it to yourself too."

"Oh, trust me for that," said Holman Sharpe. Their talk was interrupted by the little tenderfoot office boy from Administration Shack who called from the open doorway at the end of the long row of cots.

"Danville Bently, you're wanted in the office," said he.

CHAPTER XV

THE SERENADE

Danny was nervous, but he did not show it. He had never before been summoned to the office. He had thought that by keeping out of scout activities he would be safe in the refuge of self-imposed obscurity. Lost in the nondescript company of the big dormitory, and keeping as much as he could out of touch with the management he had hoped and believed that his daring stunt of impersonation would succeed.

Now, as he made his way up toward the main body of the camp, he wondered, almost tremblingly, what was amiss. Had poor little Skinny's conscience given way under the strain? No, he knew better than that. The thin cord would never break. Would he find himself face to face with the warden of Blythedale School? Or perhaps with the real Danville Bently? There is many a slip. . . .

The usual group was lolling about the steps of the official building. From his place on the railing, Roy Blakeley called, "Hey what are

103

you doing up here at the hole of holes? (meaning holy of holies). And how are things down in Pie Row? How is Sophomore, Senior, Postgraduate Sharpe these beautiful days? I hear he's going to hire a bookkeeper. Hey Bent, why don't you come up to camp once in a while so we won't forget what you look like? Don't remember to do your good turn daily.''

In the office the young clerk in khaki showed Danny into the sanctum of the powers, where he waited nervously while Councilor Wainwright finished reading a letter. ''Well my boy,'' said that official, glancing up pleasantly; ''how do you think you like camp?''

''It's one camp, all right,'' said Danny. ''It's big enough, I'll say.''

''We thought perhaps we'd hear from you—see your name up on the board or something, glorifying Florida.''

Danny winced a bit at this. ''We've got a scout down there that takes care of all those things for us,'' said he. It was this good-humored nonchalance of his which drew people to him. Discerning men construed his slightly sneering attitude to mean that he was impatient of little people and little things. The councilor chuckled appreciatively. ''It takes all kinds to make a square mile of camp,'' he said.

"Now, Bently," he continued, deliberately going to the matter in hand, "this is what I wanted to see you about. Sometimes things get around to headquarters rather late. I understand you punched a boy the first day you were here."

"Did he tell you?"

"Of course he didn't. That was a good scout you punched."

"It was a good punch I gave him."

"I heard it was. But, of course, he had just lost his temper."

"I did a good turn, I helped him to find it."

"Well, my boy, we won't go into that now. We usually find up here that a boy who is free with his fists is—well, it's a kind of a habit with him. There are those who hit and those who don't. I think I can't recall a single instance up here of a boy hitting another boy who didn't before the season was over do the same thing again. Now, honor bright, you've slugged fellows before, haven't you?"

"Sure, a guy named Kinney back in——"

"So you see. Now I just want to warn you not to do that sort of thing again. If you do, you'll go right back to Florida, Bently. This camp isn't the Madison Square Garden or the Chicago Stadium. We don't expect our guests to take the law in their own hands—ever. Of course, what I say to you applies to every boy here, and there's going to be a notice out there on the board so none of you young Jack Dempseys can come back at us. Any boy that uses his fists leaves this camp—quick. Just you read what it says in the Handbook on being a gentleman. You ever get any hints out of the Handbook?"

"There's some pretty good dope in that," said Danny.

"I'll say there is."

"And there's a lot of play-in-the-backyard stuff too."

Councilor Wainwright laughed heartily at this frank young critic. "Well, let's hear from you on some of the good stuff," said he. "You scouts down in the dormitory,—we hardly know you're alive up here. All right, my boy, no hard feelings."

Danny went out, greatly relieved. More than that, he inhaled a kind of fresh assurance that everything would be all right. Loyal little Skinny was like the Rock of Gibraltar. Blythedale Reform School was so far away. Danny felt more secure than ever in this woodland refuge. And Danville Bently, the real Danville Bently was—why, by this time he was in

Europe with his people. The only person that Danny had to fear was himself. Well, that would be all right, he would keep his fists where they belonged. No danger. He even felt that he had gained something; Councilor Wainwright seemed to like him.

But there was a black cloud on the horizon. You would not think of calling Roy Blakeley a black cloud, yet he was the black cloud in this instance. He was a boy who would sit contentedly on a fence thinking of nothing in particular, then suddenly be aroused to mirthful enterprise as by an inspiration. Surely he was one of the spirits of Temple Camp. Boys returned home in the autumn and talked of him all winter. His patrol, the Silver Foxes, shone by his own reflected light. They were (to quote the voice of Temple Camp) a bunch of jolliers.

If Danny had not been called to the office it is probable that Roy would never have conceived the mischievous idea of descending with his bantering cronies upon the defenseless Pioneer Row. But his piquant sallies to Danny upon his visit to the seat of the powers reminded him that he had neglected Pie Alley, which was his name for that lowly suburb. Roy invariably acted upon every random inspiration.

"Come on, let's go down to Pie Alley and kid the life out of Sophomore Senior, the Student Prince of scouting," said he.

"We'll tell him he's awarded a typewriter machine," said Warde Hollister.

"We'll tell him all the tests for merit badges have been changed," said Ralph Warner.

They would have been accompanied by a clamorous escort except that it was rest hour and most scouts were either asleep or reading in reclining postures in their cabins. So no one went upon this memorable expedition but Roy and two of his patrol, Ralph Warner and Warde Hollister. Reaching the big, sprawling, shingled dormitory, they serenaded the subject of their call like knights of old. They knew that Holman Sharpe would be resting. Holman did everything that was on the scout program. He was getting his money's worth.

Roy was something of a balladist and he saluted the victim with a minstrel lay:

> "Oh Sharpy, dear Sharpy, come out of the door
> The badge list is changed and there's ninety-
> six more."

This failing to arouse him they tried again.

> "Oh Sharpy, dear Sharpy, get up and come out
> And the fourth test on plumbing we'll tell
> you about."

Still again they tried to lure him with soft melody.

"Oh Sharpy, dear Sharpy, come out with scout stealth
And we'll hand you the medal for *personal health*."

Holman Sharpe did not come out, but he looked out through the open window.

CHAPTER XVI

THE ACCUSED

"Don't you scouts know it's rest hour?" said Holman. "You'd better look in your handbooks and see what's on page three thirty-seven. What are you scouts doing down here at this time of day?"

"It's a lie!" said Roy. "You can't believe a word the Handbook says—you can't even believe the punctuation. It says you can find comfort in the woods and we looked all around and didn't find any—we even used our searchlights, I'll leave it to Warde. Hey, Sharpy, come on out, the National Council has decided that a hobby-horse isn't an animal so you can't name a patrol after it. Honest, I'll leave it to Ralph Warner. You can't press the leaves of a hat-tree either—there's a new rule—so if you have any you better throw them away. The rules are all changed, you can't get the printing badge by finding footprints any more. Hey, come on out, Sharpy."

Holman did not immediately respond to this merry summons, but Danny who was in the dormitory strolled out smiling and sat on the steps. Holman's methodical activities amused him, but he had never poked fun at him.

"Hey, Florida," said Roy; "how 'bout it— isn't it true they're going to give crutches for veteran scouts? You better put in your application while you're young, Sharpy. You better start saving up."

Holman emerged upon the porch. There was nothing sissified about this boy; it was not for that reason that they took delight in "jollying" him. It was that he was so terribly sober and earnest. He was going to be a scout by the book; he thought that if he could pass an examination in scouting he would be a scout. He was studying it, cramming, and he thought that boys who were just naturally scouts and did not study it very hard, were slackers.

Roy had fifteen merit badges and had enjoyed the fun of getting them. But this serious boy was not having the time of his life being a scout. He should have been at boarding school, where he would have won honors. Handbooks and tests and awards will help, of course, but scouting is a matter of fine spirit. The scout who thinks only of getting ahead, of swimming fifty yards because the book prescribes it, is apt to forget about his comrade scouts.

A curriculum is a pretty poor sort of a pal.

"I should think you scouts would know this is rest hour," said Holman. "If you want to get anywhere in scouting you've got to relax. You come around here with your nonsense when I'm supposed to be storing up a little energy."

"Tell us all about that," encouraged Ralph Warner, winking at Danny, who was highly amused.

"On account of your yelling I'll have to make it up to-morrow when I ought to be stalking," said Holman.

"There may be some truth in that," teased Warde. "Hey, Sharpy, why don't you go out on a hike with your friend and neighbor some night for no reason at all?"

"With Bently, you mean? I'd never accomplish much. I guess he's a sort of more of a tramp than a scout. I'd never learn much from him. I've only got eight weeks here."

"You let him say that about you, Florida?" Warde asked.

"Sure, let him go as far as he likes," laughed Danny. "I don't claim to be a scout."

"I don't see what you're here for then?" said Holman.

"I can tell you the reason," said Roy. "He's here because he's here. Am I right, Florida?"

"Surest thing," laughed Danny. He was hugely entertained as he sat on the steps watching this show.

"He's wasting his father's money," said Holman. "If that's any comfort to him."

"How do you know his father's got any money?" Warde shot back.

"He deduced it by deduction," said Danny.

"If he'll let me help him on scout stuff, I'll be glad to do it," said Holman.

"There's your chance, Florida," Warde and Ralph shouted together.

"I don't believe I could make the grade," said Danny.

"You could if you tried; you don't try," said Holman.

"Hey, Sharpy," said Roy, "there's something we came here to see you about. Let's quit fooling. These two silver-plated foxes and myself were appointed a committee to come here and ascertain—did you get that word, *ascertain?* We have to find out if it's true what all the fellows are saying that you went down to Catskill with Tom Slade in his Ford and then came back and said that you crossed Valley Creek by means of a ford and then claimed the *new discovery prize* on account of finding a way to get over Valley Creek not by the bridge.

If you did that it was dishonest and conduct unbecoming to a scout. Are you claiming that prize or not? Yes or no—or both. Did you deliberately accidentally deceive the Council or not?''

''You'd better look out how you talk about dishonesty and deceiving,'' said Holman rather heatedly.

''I call your attention to law one on page something or other of the Scout Handbook,'' Roy persisted.

''That's the wrong page,'' said Warde.

''Then it's page sumpty-sump,'' said Roy. ''A scout's honor is to be toasted—trusted. If he violates his honor by telling a lie—comma— or cheating—comma—he may be directed other- wise told to hand over his scout badge—period. Holman Sharpe of Pie Alley, if you did that we demand that you hand over your scout badge to this committee of solid-silver foxes. Lying cannot be tolerated in Temple Camp—unless you're lying down so as to relax and store up energy.''

By this time Danny was laughing aloud; there was just the faintest suggestion of Skinny about his countenance when he laughed. But Hol- man Sharpe was clearly ruffled and he ad- vanced, not exactly menacingly, but with something in his manner which showed that he did not at all catch the humor of their reference to dishonesty and deception. He was a serious and literal boy and construed the use of these words in any case as a slur and an insult.

"You said something about a scout's honor," he said. "It's on page thirty-four if you want to know where it is. You better look out how you talk about mine. The first thing you scouts know, one of you will get what he good and plenty deserves." Granted, this boy knew a good deal about scouting; but he did not know much about scouts.

"If I said anything I'm sorry for, I'm glad of it," said Ralph.

"Well you said—your leader said that lying isn't tolerated at this camp. That's as much as calling me a liar." Now he did advance, flushed and angry.

"Cut it out," said Roy good-naturedly, seeing which way the tide was setting.

"As long as you spoke of a scout's honor—" Holman began.

"Cut it out, you blamed simp," said Ralph, his tone changing suddenly to disgust.

"I'll remind you of law ten,* too," said Holman.

* This law refers to bravery and standing up for the right.

"Yere, we know all about it," said Ralph. "Don't tell us about scouting. We were here before you ever heard of this camp. You better learn to take a joke——"

"Sure, that's another law," said Roy.

"And as long as you're making such a fuss about lying," said Ralph contemptuously, "if you want me to make you out a liar, I'll do it. How about calling Florida a tramp? Who the dickens do you think you are, calling scouts tramps? *Wasting his father's money;* can you beat that? *Gee,* as long as you want to be serious, I'll say you were lying."

This was intended more as a compliment to Danny, whom they all seemed to like, than as a slur to Holman. Certainly nothing was further from the minds of these young Silver Foxes than to start a quarrel. But the serious Holman always carried his "honor" around with him as he did his field book. He chose to take Ralph's remark as an insult and he struck him more from a sense of duty than from anger.

Scarcely did the astonished Ralph realize what had happened when Danny sprang between, spreading his arms to separate the two. "That's enough, cut it out," he said. But indeed there was no chance of a fight. Holman having done his duty stalked into the dormitory. Warde and Roy, highly aroused by his act, followed him protesting. So there for the moment stood Ralph, his hand against his face with Danny standing before him saying, "That's enough, no more."

Just at that moment Councilor Wainwright, carrying his big flat chart book and inspection record, came around the corner of the building and paused suddenly.

"At it again, Bently?" he queried with grim cordiality.

CHAPTER XVII

THE MASQUERADER

The councilor did not wait for an answer. "Not hurt much?" he commented rather than asked. "Suppose you come along to the office with me, Bently."

To Ralph Warner's astonishment, Danny accompanied the councilor without so much as a word. When Warde and Roy presently reappeared, there stood Ralph recovering from his surprise rather than from the hurt, which was not serious.

"He won't come out," said Warde, referring to Holman. "He did his duty—can you beat it? Where's Florida?"

"Gone with Wainey," said Ralph. "He went before I knew it. I guess Wainey thinks he did it."

"What did he want to go for?" Roy asked.

"Search me," Ralph answered.

"Come on, don't bother about Sharpy," said Warde. "Gee, I'm sorry Wainey had to come along just then. Honest, isn't that just like him?"

"Can you beat it?" Roy asked. "If the world should come to an end, he'd sure be the first one there. Jiminies, Ralph, don't be sore, it wasn't Sharpy hitting you, it was the Scout Handbook."

"Sure," laughed Warde.

"I understand," Ralph agreed. "Gee, that feller must be crazy."

"He's troubled with static," said Roy; "come on, let's beat it."

None of the three of them had the least notion that Florida, as they called him, was deliberately posing as the culprit. Councilor Wainwright's threatened warning had never appeared on the bulletin board and the three Silver Foxes did not apprehend any very serious sequel to the little affair. They supposed that the councilor did not intend to take notice of it; certainly not to act upon it at that time. They inferred that he wished to see Danny about something else, and encountering him by chance, had asked him to go along. That was the way they saw it, and they thought no more about it. Or if they did, it was in a way of humorous dismay at Holman Sharpe's unexpected conduct. You may say they were not ideal scouts. You may, if you choose, say that Holman *was* a true scout. Those are matters of opinion. In any event, Roy and his comrades cherished no malice. "Only there ought to be a badge for that," said Roy; "the slugger's badge. Otherwise, Sharpy will think he wasted his time. Forget it. He saw his duty and he did it nobly. I hope young Snoopy, the boy councilor, forgets it."

But Councilor Wainwright was very far from forgetting it. En route to Administration Shack he said what he had to say and it was a model of cordial brevity. "Well, my boy, you'd better pack up and get started; you know what I told you. And we won't have any explanations, eh? It seems you and I don't understand each other—no hard feelings. Maybe we'll hear of you as a heavyweight champion some day. Let's see, you were paid up for the month, I think?"

"That'll be O. K.," said Danny.

"What was it, another one on the eye?" the councilor asked cheerily, as he hurried along. You would have thought him a fight fan.

"N—not so good," said Danny, "I've done better."

"Well, now you see Temple Camp can make good its threats too."

"Fifty-fifty," said Danny. "Don't aim unless you'll shoot."

"That's the idea," said the Councilor, in great good humor. Danny rather liked this man who was as good as his word; he had a sportsman's respect for him. For Danny was always as good as his word. Scout or not, he was that.

In the office the business was very brief. Up to the point of judgment Temple Camp was easy-going. But after that the procedure was summary. The board of the absent Danville Bently had, as we know, been paid by check for the month of July. The letter from Florida which Danny had found and destroyed, shifted this payment to cover the month of August. It was now the middle of July and Danny had used up two weeks' value of Mr. Roswell Bently's money. The unused balance of thirty dollars together with forty dollars to make up the amount of his transportation home, was given to him, and this extra forty was billed to his supposed parent.

Thus, after two weeks of masquerading, this escaped inmate of a reform school stood expelled from Temple Camp wearing a scout suit and with seventy dollars in his pocket.

With the same nonchalant air that had made him a leader at Blythedale School he ambled out of the office and back toward Pioneer Row.

Seeing Roy and his two companions near the wig-wag tower he strolled over to them. His pace was random, his general demeanor idle. He had that about him which seemed to say that nothing was of very much importance; a kind of sneering sophistication. By the record he was certainly not a good boy. When he did a good thing it was with a certain appearance of mockery at goodness. He had not much use for the fuss and feathers of scouting.

"Hey, you guys," said he, pausing in a kind of half-interested way. "Can you all keep your mouths shut? That little racket is all over; see? Keep away from the office and those bosses. No matter what—keep your mouths shut."

"Was Wainey talking to you about it?" Warde asked.

"Now what did I say about keeping your mouth shut?"

"Is he going to jump on Sharpy?" Ralph asked. "Gee whiz, I don't want him to."

"For what?" Danny asked. "Sharpy didn't slam you, you only dreamed it. Forget it. None of us know anything about it. Nobody's going to talk to you and you don't have to talk to anybody. It's all settled. If you want to pull the scout stuff now's your chance. Nobody's going to talk to you about it, so just keep your mouths shut. Go on down to the lake and kid somebody along and forget it.''

It was odd how silent and respectful they were, these boys who were never able to keep still. They did not even pester him with questions. Somehow they felt that this boy, who had not a single scout achievement to his credit, was their superior. ''Sure we won't,'' Warde said.

''Don't make a lot out of nothing,'' said Danny, as he walked away.

He ambled down to Pioneer Row and into the big dormitory. He had been told to get his things, but of course, he had no things to get. He strolled down the aisle between the cots till he came to the one on which Holman Sharpe was propped up, reading. In the interval since the altercation the bell had rung and the rest period being over the place was rapidly deserted. Only Holman remained in the big bare place, engrossed with his clerical labors. Danny rather disrespectfully threw a book or two out of the way and kicked another to the floor, clearing a place so that he could sit on the foot of the cot and talk.

''That the English one?'' he asked, poking Sir Baden-Powell's book idly with his foot. ''Never mind, let it alone; won't hurt it to be on the floor. How you feeling, Harpo-Sharpo?"

"I'm just finishing; I'm going to take my twenty yard swim this afternoon."

"Can't swim the lake yet, huh?"

"No, but I will."

"Sure you will. Listen here, professor. They've got some kind of darn crazy rule in this summer resort about scrapping. Not that you're a scrapper, because you don't know how to hit. They're putting up a notice about it, I understand. If they find out you passed one to that feller—what's his name—they'll can you. It's not a part of the game. You can stick out your tongue at a scout, but you can't paste him. That's the only thing I know about scouting, but I know that. You can take that one lesson from me. So as long as I'm not a boy scout anyway—I mean a regular feller like you—I'm going to be the one that hit foxy silver polish or whatever his name is. You get the idea? I'm only here for two weeks more anyway, and you've got work enough on hand to keep you here till New Year's. On the dead level I don't see how you're ever going to get away with it unless you cash in on that astronomy stuff and eat your meals by deduction. So I'm starting——"

"You mean you're going to take the blame?"

"Sure, I haven't got anything else to take away with me. I suppose I'm entitled to a little disgrace if I want it. Now—now, just a minute! You have to do your good turn, don't you? All right, now don't go shouting about your upper cut—it was a punk hit anyway— and you're all hunk here till they close the show or your health breaks down from over study. You see I'm not losing anything, be- cause I'm not booked up for rewards. Now I've got those silver gold dust triplets or what- ever you call 'em, fixed. All you have to do is just remember that you had a dream about slugging a boy scout. So long, Sharpy, old scout, and good luck to you."

CHAPTER XVIII

TO PASTURES NEW

One might suppose that such a boy as Danny would have at least the quality of understanding himself; he was nonchalant and self-assured; so easily the master of a situation. But strangely enough, now that he had plenty of money and could go upon his way with comparative safety, he felt neither safe nor comfortable. He had suffered no scruples at masquerading at the expense of an unknown scout, but now that the unused balance of this board money was handed him, he felt like a thief. Such is the strange quality of money! There are those who will accept favors of every sort, except money. As long as he had been a guest (?) at camp he had not thought of himself as doing anything dishonest. Risky no doubt, but not *stealing*. But now his act was reduced to its common denominator. He held the money, not simply what the money represented. And he felt exactly as if he had stolen it. It needed only these crisp bills to remind him of the out-

rageous fraud he had been perpetrating.
—Money to return to Florida.

This climax of affairs troubled him, for it
showed him that he was not so sure of himself.
In a way, Temple Camp had found him out, or
at least revealed him to himself. He had
avoided scouting so as to keep under cover.
Then he had deliberately sauntered to his own
destruction by accepting the dismissal which
should have been Holman Sharpe's. That is,
he had done a good turn, which of course, is
scouting. In the course of this renunciation
he had found himself in possession of seventy
dollars. And he could not keep it. He was
thoroughly annoyed with himself at this. He
was found out—he had found himself out.
He had tracked himself and found himself. He
alone had done the whole business!

"They must think I'm joy riding in a baby
carriage, needing money," he said to himself.
He was not willing to put his act of returning
the money on the somewhat weak and "kid-
dish" grounds of honesty. Such a resourceful,
skillful boy as he, could travel without money.
And so forth and so on. Anyway, he sauntered
with his finest nonchalant air into Administration Shack, giving a little sneery look at the
stuffed birds and snake skins displayed there.

He could never, *never* go in for scouting. Oh
no! He pulled out one of the chairs around the
big writing table, sat down, pulled a Temple
Camp envelope to him, put the money into it
and addressed it, "To the Managers of Temple Camp."

He scaled it over to the young clerk at the
desk as he went out. "Here's a love letter for
Wainey and the bunch," he said. "Tell 'em
I didn't need it."

"Sorry you're going, Scout Bently," said
the young scout clerk.

"That's all right, so long, old man."

"You'll find it pretty hot in Florida this time
of year, won't you?"

"I'm not there yet."

"You going down on the bus?"

"No, I'm going to hike down and get the six
thirty-two."

"Well, hope to see you again."

One thing he wanted to do and that was to
find Skinny. Poor Skinny, he would be relieved
by the departure of this unconcerned young
masquerader. In that two weeks he had obeyed
Danny's order and not sought him out. He
had smiled shyly on the two or three occasions
when they had passed each other by and once
at night, when all the scouts were at camp-

fire, he had ventured down to the deserted
Pioneer Row to have just a few words with his
dubious hero if Danny were there. But he
could not find him. "He's scared, because he
thinks maybe I look like him," Skinny said to
himself. As if he, Skinny, could look like that
resourceful and daring adventurer! He had
thought much about Danny, and worried about
him, in those two weeks. Once he had seen a
strange man coming along the path west of the
storehouse holding a boy by the collar and he
had been seized with panic fear that it was
Danny in the clutch of the Blythedale authorities, until he saw that it was just a visiting
parent indulging in pleasantries with his son.

But Skinny was not to be found on that afternoon of Danny's sudden departure, and
Danny took the trail around the lake without
seeing him. He went that way because he
wished to avoid villages and the open roads.
The route was longer and much more difficult
than that via the highroad, but he could get to
Catskill without passing through Leeds. His
intention was to hook a ride on a train to New
York and then, having no money, to use his
wits. But, of course, Danny never knew from
one minute to another what he would do.

So Holman Sharpe was able to proceed uninterrupted with his strenuous cramming in the interest of scouting. We should not be too severe with Holman. Realizing what Danny was doing for his sake, he tried to find him and insist that they tell Councilor Wainwright the truth. But Danny had already gone. That was the great thing about Danny, he was always as good as his word and acted promptly. Whether it was hitting a boy in the eye or making a sacrifice, it was all the same. He hated talk and posing.

Thus baffled in his effort to make amends, Holman contented himself with the comfortable view that after all his "studies" were more important than the unprofitable loitering of a boy like Danny. Making good use of one's time was surely the paramount virtue, greater than generosity and sacrifice. We shall meet Holman again some day and it will be interesting to note how his studious concentration worked out. He cared more for scouting than he did for scouts.

Nor should we be too lenient with Danny. He had a kind of sophisticated contempt for the prescribed routine of scouting and it was not exactly in the spirit of self-sacrifice that he saved Holman from summary dismissal. It amused him and annoyed him to see this smug candidate for scout honors delving in books and planning to do things which he, Danny, could do so easily. As long as Holman liked that sort of baby play, Danny was quite ready to assure him his continuance of it. But it was with a tolerant sneer that he did it. And generous acts are not done with a sneer.

Moreover, Danny knew that in a couple of weeks the real Danville Bently would arrive and a crisis occur. He had done his stunt of masquerading, and had been able thus to lie low in the perilous days following his escape from the reform school. He went away owing Temple Camp (or the real Bently) the amount of two weeks board, but he had balked at taking the cash that had been proffered him, and had gone penniless.

It may be added that he succeeded in finding the trail through the mountain pass across the lake, which Holman Sharpe had tried four times to follow in doing test four for the first class scout badge.

CHAPTER XIX

THE NEW ARRIVAL

Perhaps poor little Skinny's big eyes stared a little more than usual on his hearing of Danny's departure. But he did not fear for Danny. He knew that Danny was equal to anything, that he led a charmed life. He did not know why Danny had left (nobody seemed to know that) but he was not greatly surprised. Back home, Danny had always been the true free lance, coming and going at will. He had followed a circus as far as Ohio and come safely home. To Skinny he was superhuman. Down in that stout little heart, Danny, with all his dubious qualities, was the real hero. He could do anything he wanted to do. All that troubled Skinny was that he wanted to do such dreadful things.

Early on the afternoon of August Second he trembled as a little group of new arrivals came down the woods path from the road where the bus had set them down. He stood, a poor, shabby little figure, on the porch of Administration Shack watching those khaki clad boys with suit-cases and duffel bags, as they were piloted into the office. He was just the queer little mascot of camp, a law unto himself, and no longer bothered because he did not wear the scout regalia. They took him around with them, rowing and hiking, because of a superstition that he brought good luck. Sometimes they took him out in the canoe that he had won in an insane frenzy, and he was always shyly pleased to go. Ask any scout in camp about that phenomenal exploit and he would tell you that Skinny did it in a fit and could never do it again. But he was always on hand on Administration porch to gaze at new arrivals. He was the court fool, the camp pet, always in evidence, staring in amazement at the great world.

Among these new arrivals on that day was a tall, merry faced boy, whose natty scout suit set off his trim, slender form. He was distinguishable from the others (a patrol and a two patrol troop) by a spotless white scout scarf which, instead of being tied in a knot was drawn through a wide silver ring. His belt was white, too, a noticeable variation in the scout raiment. He climbed to the porch rather hesitatingly behind the others, but he was not embarrassed at the patrol of authority, for he gave Skinny a funny wink which aroused

the little fellow to eager laughter. When
Skinny laughed the skin of his thin face tightened about his mouth, giving the appearance
of an older person's smile, but his big eager
eyes redeemed this rather pitiful effect.

"What's the white scarf for?" he ventured
to ask upon the strength of that pleasant wink.

"Polar Bears of Florida," said the boy.

"They don't have polar bears in Florida,"
Skinny ventured.

"No, that's the funny part of it," the boy
laughed.

Skinny did not realize till this boy had gone
inside that he was the real Danville Bently of
Wave Crest City, Florida. He did not venture
into the office for there was a rug on the floor
and somehow he was always timid where there
were rugs. But he stood at the window looking in. He wondered if something involving
himself would now happen. His nerves were
all on edge. There would be an explosion, he
thought. The tall boy stood aside waiting till
the others were enrolled. Skinny felt that this
was for a purpose. The boy looked very conspicuous in there with his white scarf and belt
in striking contrast to his khaki attire. Skinny
now noticed that the hat he held had a white
cord on it also. He seemed to be waiting just

from politeness, but Skinny's little hands trembled in panic excitement.

The others emerged, singly and in groups, and now the tall boy was at the counter. There was evidently some trouble and the clerk began running through a card catalogue. Councilor Tenny was called and together the three talked at the counter. Then Tom Slade, the young camp assistant, appeared among them. Pretty soon he began laughing and Skinny was relieved. The new boy laughed too. But Councilor Tenny did not laugh. He shook his head as if puzzled. Then they got a letter and read it. Pretty soon the new boy came out laughing.

"Well *you* don't have to worry," Tom called after him. "But it's blamed funny we never got that letter."

"I know my name if I don't know anything else," laughed the boy. "I wish I was as sure of my first class badges as I am of my—what d'you call it—identity?"

"Beats me," said Tom, pausing on the steps. "All right, Bently, don't worry; we like mysteries here."

"I'll write to my dad and he'll straighten it out," the boy said.

"This is a great place, Bent, we have dark and bloody mysteries," said Tom. "Long as

you know who you are, you're all right. Get
busy—eats at six.'' That was just his off-hand,
hearty way with new arrivals.

So the worst was over and Skinny had not
been torn to pieces or struck dead. Temple
Camp survived the dreadful fraud. Tom
Slade had even laughed; he loved so to have
a joke on the office.

''Will you let me show you where you're
going to go?'' Skinny asked. ''Are you going
to the dormitory? I'll show you. 'Cause my
patrol went on a hike, so I'll show you.''

''I'm going to Tent Village, wherever that
is?''

''I'll show you—it's dandy there. Is your
name—what's your name?'' he asked, hurrying
along by the new boy's side.

''Danville Bently.''

''Have you got a patrol?''

''Sure, but I don't carry it around with me;
I just came from Europe. A chap was here
for a couple of weeks and gave my name, that's
what all the fuss was about. Nobody seems
to know anything about him.''

''Will—they won't catch him, will they?''

''If he was slick enough to do that, I guess
they won't if you're asking me.''

''He was smart, hey? Even if he wasn't

maybe kind of a hero, he was smart, hey?"

"There have been lots of worse ones; look at Robin Hood."

"Even he was bad, but he was a hero, hey?"

"I'd kind of like to know who he was. I hope I'll turn out to be as smart as he is."

"You're not mad at him?" Skinny asked.

"I never get mad at anybody. My dad's the one that loses, and he'll have a good laugh over it."

"Why do you wear white? It looks awful different?"

"Why do kids ask questions?"

"You're a second class scout?" Skinny asked, noticing the badge.

"I'll be a first class one in a few days or I'll kick myself. Have you got seven miles around here that you're not using, so I can hike it?"

"That's in test four," Skinny said. "Do you want me to go for a witness?"

"Sure, you're always welcome."

"I know a good test four hike and I can always go, because mostly my patrol are away doing all kinds of things. I can always go— if you want me to. I won the Hiawatha canoe for swimming across the lake; I'll show it to you, but most of the time it's out."

"Ever hear of Dutch Henny's Cave?"

"Sure I did. I bet you read about it in the Temple Camp booklet, hey? It's just seven miles. I'll show you Spook Falls too, because they make a noise like crying at night. That's a good test five hike for second class, because it's just a mile; they go scout pace."

"How 'bout twelve on the first?"

"You mean getting a new scout? That's hard, because they're all scouts up here. If you ask me things, I can tell you."

"Good."

"Now we're coming to Tent Village," said Skinny. "It's good it's all full in Pioneer Dormitory, so they don't put you there. Can I be special friends with you? Are you going to get prizes and awards?"

"Search *me;* I'm going to get a lot of fun," said Danville Bently.

CHAPTER XX

SKINNY'S PROTÉGÉ

The next day a notice somewhat more lengthy and conspicuous than the usual hastily written announcements appeared on the big bulletin board at Administration Shack. It was typewritten and signed by the two resident trustees. Skinny gazed at it, appalled.

The management of Temple Camp is mortified to make known that the honorable uniform of scouting has been lately used to perpetrate a gross and criminal fraud in this community. On July First a boy representing himself to be a scout, enrolled and secured assignment to quarters at this office. He registered the name of Danville Bently of Florida, a scout who was expected at that time. This unknown boy was lately dismissed from camp for sufficient reasons at the end of two weeks enjoyment of the camp's hospitality. A letter, deferring the arrival of the true Danville Bently, failed to be received at this office and was probably intercepted.

The management of this camp has regretfully had occasion to warn its guests against canvassers representing themselves to be connected with the movement, but never heretofore against any one wrongfully impersonating a scout.

Loyalty to this camp and jealousy for the honor of the scout uniform, will prompt any one who has

any knowledge or suspicions of the whereabouts and
identity of this miscreant, promptly to bring same
to the attention of the management.

This certainly set the matter forth in its true
colors and Skinny was aghast. What would
they say if they knew that this "miscreant"
was also a fugitive from a reform school? But
the affair was over and he would not worry
any more about it. The bulletin was just a random shot in the dark and nothing happened.
Danny was safe. No one knew Danny as he
did or they would not put out such notices.

He became devoted to Danville Bently. The
only way that Skinny could make friends with
a boy was to catch him early, before he was
drawn into the activities of the camp life.
Every newcomer had a rather slow day or two
before becoming acquainted, and this was particularly so with boys who came without their
troops. After a new boy became involved in
the camp life, he saw Skinny simply as the
little mascot and was content to "jolly" him
as every one else did. He was not likely to
take this queer little fellow seriously and to
make a pal of him. Skinny knew this from
bitter experience and he capitalized his knowledge of camp and the neighboring countryside
with every new arrival. New boys were glad

enough to hobnob with this eager little guide while there was nothing else to do and had no scruples about deserting him as soon as they were drawn into the camp life. Skinny knew that he must strike while the iron was hot, as the saying is, and he was always to be found, a gaunt little figure, waiting on Administration steps when the bus came in. No boy could possibly dislike Skinny. But on the other hand no boy could possibly make a permanent comrade of him.

But Danville Bently did just that. The contrast between Skinny and himself was ridiculous, but he seemed not to notice it. A boy who deliberately chose Skinny's company was apt to get himself laughed at. But no one dreamed of laughing. Perhaps no one dared to laugh at this tall boy with the white scarf and belt who ambled about with the cadaverous little gnome who took such conspicuous delight in his company. Once again Skinny had done the unexpected and won a real prize. Truly indeed he never did anything on a small scale.

At first the camp paid no attention while this shabby little janitor showed the new tenant around the enchanted place. That was Skinny's customary job. But when Howell Cross, of the First Vermont Eagles (and an

Eagle Scout) asked Danville to go on a point hike and he pleasantly declined, the big heroes of Temple Camp began to sit up and take notice.

"Sorry," said he, "but I'm going out on the lake with Alfred McCord. Tell your patrol I appreciate their asking me." Howell and the others who stood by were astonished not only because it was a compliment to the new boy for the Eagle Patrol so to honor him, but because none of them had ever before heard Skinny called by his real name Alfred. They were to hear that name a good deal in the future.

"Can't you go out on the lake with him any day?" one of these scouts asked.

"Sure, so why not to-day?" said Danville. "It's up to you."

"How do you like it in Tent Village?"

"All right."

"If you don't like it with the singles you can be a season member of my patrol," said Eagle Scout Cross. "I'm one short, he's away with his folks. They let you do that up here, you know."

"Oh, he knows," laughed another scout. "I guess little sqeedunk told him everything."

"He never told me he stole the white pennant," said Danville not unpleasantly, but with just a touch of sharpness.

It was the first time these well known scouts of camp had come face to face with the tall boy with the soft southern accent, and they observed him closely. They were all scouts of achievement; the Vermont Eagles were a crack patrol and Howell Cross, their leader, was a hero with a following. There were, alas, drones at camp, but this circle was finely representative of scouting. They saw nothing about Bently to suggest the laggard or slacker, or mere "guest" at camp. He had what even Howell Cross had not, and that was a certain picturesqueness; but it was of a sort that revealed no crink or cranny where boyish ridicule could penetrate. An odd hat, or even too much attention to ostentatious details of scout attire (shades of Pee-wee Harris) was pretty sure to arouse mirth and banter in this big community. But the full white scarf with belt and hat cord to match, worn by this tall, self-possessed boy, excited no humorous comment. They asked him respectfully about it.

"Polar Bears," said he. "And I know there aren't any in Florida and that's the funny part. I bet I've said that fifty times since I came here."

"We can sure tell you a long way off," said Howell pleasantly. "Does the silver ring mean anything?"

"It only means my sister gave it to me when I joined the scouts."

"Gee, it's nifty all right. It's not a patrol ring?"

"Yes it is, we all got them."

"You don't have to tie it in a knot, gee that's good."

Ordinarily the mention of a sister would have given Temple Camp just the chance it loved. They would have used the sister to belittle their victim. They would have said, "Oh joy, he's got a little sister." But they just were not moved to do that. They looked at his white scarf gathered into the shining silver ring, and at his belt, and everything about him. They were interested, respectful. And a trifle puzzled. That he should have an engagement with Skinny McCord! And that he seemed to have every intention of keeping it, just as if it were a *real* engagement.

CHAPTER XXI

TEMPLE CAMP TAKES NOTICE

They even lingered in group form, watching him as he ambled off down toward the lake. He had been at camp nearly a week, and he was still quietly devoted to Skinny. He had not exploited Skinny nor made any ostentatious show of being his champion. Yet he was devoted to him in an easy-going unpretentious sort of way. He had never said, nor even thought, "I might as well be nice to the poor kid." Evidently he did not know that Skinny was just a poor little codger—a mascot. Somebody would have to tell him about that. The funny part of it was that he did not get himself laughed at.

Skinny's winning of the Hiawatha canoe had not brought him any lasting glory. The white pennant had been lifted many times since he had scampered off with it, eager and trembling. But now scouts began to wonder how he had secured this permanent award of the tall, polite, easy-going boy with the white scarf. They did not exactly begin to take Skinny seriously, but they were puzzled. They tried to find a weak point in Bently, some idle or effeminate quality, but there was just nothing to get hold of.

Skinny was waiting at the lake, eager and anxious. He lived in perpetual dread that Bently would "fall down" on him. But Bently never did. He came ambling down with that pleasant smile which always reassured Skinny.

"Did they ask you to go on bee-line with them?"

"Point to point, you mean?"

"Yes, they call it bee-line for short. I never went on one, but I know all about how they do; you have to go across brooks and climb over things and everything; you'd have a lot of fun. That feller that was kidding me at camp-fire last night—you know that fat feller?—he went through a house, even. Are you sure you're going to go out with me?"

"I ought to be the one to know," said Danville.

"Did they try to get you to not do it?"

"No, why? How are we going; in your canoe?"

"Yes, but it's out, my patrol is using it. Maybe we better take a boat, hey? That's it, over in the middle of the lake."

"Seems to be coming in, let's wait for it."

They sat down on the springboard to wait. The lake was dotted with boats; every one seemed to be out fishing.

"I couldn't swim across again, because I was crazy that time," said Skinny.

"You can do things when you're crazy," Danville said.

"*I* can," said Skinny, "but not any other time. I got to get all crazy like. Do you? It don't count so much if you're crazy like. That's why everybody forgot about it. They said I was lucky."

"They said that about Lindbergh."

"If I get good and mad, then I can do things. Only most of the time I can't get mad. They're nice to me up here, that's sure."

"Yes, that's good."

"Are we going to stay friends like? I don't mean just jollying me, but are we going to stay friends like this?"

"Why not?"

"Because I'm a mascot. Do you mind if I don't have a regular scout suit?"

"I never noticed."

"Here they come now, they're coming in. That feller paddling in front is Hunt Ward. That other one paddling is Connie Bennett, he's my patrol leader. That other one belongs in a troop from Rhode Island; he goes around with them a lot; he likes my patrol.''

The Hiawatha canoe, with its merry trio, glided toward the float, Connie brought it around, and it paused rocking alongside. ''H'lo Skinny,'' Hunt called.

''Can I go out in it now?'' Skinny asked. ''This feller's going with me, can I use it?''

They glanced at Danville who stood by, watching them. ''You ought to have been down here an hour ago,'' Hunt said to him, ''and you could have gone along. We've got some perch.''

''Now is just as good,'' said Danville.

''She's all full of water, wait till we get her on the float and tip her,'' Connie said.

The three voyagers proceeded with the rather clumsy task of hauling the canoe up on the float and turning it over.

''You don't need to haul her up,'' Danville said. ''Here, let me show you.''

He kneeled on the float, and reached over, pulling the opposite gunwale up and toward him. By a quick application of dexterity and strength the canoe was tipped up sideways against the edge of the float, and the water poured out of it. Then Danville eased it down into the lake again. By this trick he did a two man job while the others stood watching and feeling a little superfluous. Yet it was more than a trick, for when Connie tried to do the same thing he could not with all his strength raise the canoe to the necessary angle. "That's some wrinkle," he said. He preferred to view it as a trick rather than as an exhibition of extraordinary strength. "I guess you've got to know how," he said.

"Oh, yes," laughed Danville.

They had intended to jolly Skinny and discourage his project of using the canoe. The Elks thought a good deal of this canoe. They liked to see it safely in its locker when they were not using it. They had intended to say as usual, "Oh, you don't want to use it." But here was an embarrassing complication. The tall, smiling boy with the white scarf had modestly shown them a trick and a strength of arm not to be ridiculed. This was no time or place for authority or banter. He was quite master of the situation. It would be quite absurd to remind Skinny of dangers.

"I suppose it's all right for us to go out in his canoe, isn't it?" Danville asked. There was no hint of sarcasm in his remark and his handsome open face was wreathed in a friendly smile. But just the same these Elks felt a rebuke. A strange, uncomfortable feeling was upon them that this boy was their master, mentally and physically. If they had been sure that he meant that pronoun *his* in a sneering sense, they could have got back at him. But they did not know what he meant, any more than they knew how he had tipped the canoe. They were wise scouts and they made no mistake. Somehow or other no boys ever made a mistake with Danville Bently. They sensed something. They were embarrassed—and respectful.

"Sure, it's his. Why can't he use it if he wants to?" Connie said. He seemed inclined to be reasonable.

"That'll be dandy," said Danville.

Just as Howell Cross's group had watched him rather puzzled, so now these three returning voyagers lingered there on the float watching him as he paddled away with Skinny wedged up in the bow like an uncanny little doll. He paddled, as he did everything else, without the slightest fuss or effort. He had that about him which suggested that he could make up his mind without the slightest fuss or effort, that he would jump off a roof without the slightest fuss or effort.

"I can't make *that* guy out," said the scout from Rhode Island. "Gee, that white scarf looks plain out on the water huh?"

"Notice how he holds his left hand?" said Connie. "I think he compensates with his right wrist, honest."

"No, it's the long back sweep," said Hunt. "Geeeee! Look at the reach he's got!"

"He kind of reminded us it was Skinny's canoe," said Connie. "Did you notice how nice he did that?"

"Sure, and he paddles the same way," laughed Hunt. "He *does* things the same way he *says* things. You never know what he means. Looks easy till you try to do it."

"Any other scout came up here with a bib around his neck they'd kid the life out of him," said Connie.

"Nothing about him looks like a bib to me," said the scout from Rhode Island.

CHAPTER XXII

PARTNERS

"Just flop around, hey?"

"Yes, that's the way I like to do," said
Skinny. "If I was in the bow of a rowboat I
couldn't look at you, because you'd be facing
backwards. I like to look at you with your
white scarf. I like canoes better than row-
boats, don't you?"

"They're not so good for dancing or scrapping."

"That's the way you talk, and it's why fellows can't make you out," said the simple
Skinny.

"Well, as long as you can make me out it's
all right," said Danville. "How 'bout it, are
you going to help me?"

"Will you let me? You mean getting your
first class badge? Are you going to do it?"

"Might as well, hadn't I?"

"And that's all you've got to do? I mean
just test four?"

"N—no, I've got two things to do," said
Danville as he paddled idly, occasionally let-

ting the paddle drip. "This scouting is a blamed nuisance."

"Now I can tell you're fooling. Kind of sometimes you remind me of my brother, only he's only a half a brother. Anyway, you're not so fresh like he is. He gets in a lot of trouble being reckless."

"That's the way to do it," said Danville. "Where's the other half of him?"

"I mean we got different mothers," said Skinny. "Once a feller got fresh with me and he knocked him kerplunk. Another feller——"

He was about to stumble into a reference to Danny's pugilistic exploit at camp, but caught himself just in time. He could not trust himself talking about Danny, and it made him feel false and dishonorable, so he changed the subject.

"Only just one test you've got to take to be in the first class? Two, you said two."

"Yep, the other's missionary stuff, training a boy to be a tenderfoot—*twelve*. I'm not so stuck on twelve except when it's twelve gumdrops for a cent. You don't happen to know any boys that want to be trained as tenderfoots or feets, whatever it is? I suppose we might kidnap one from a farm. But first how about Test Four? Tell me about that seven mile hike,

or if it turns out to be any more than seven
miles the boy scouts will have to give me a
rebate. I've been climbing up the Alps this
summer and I'm tired.''

"Those are in Europe, hey?''

"And they're up in the air—in Switzerland.
Where is this lion's den or whatever you call
it? Maybe I could go in a taxi. I've got to do
it before my dad comes up or I won't be able to
stick him for a pony next winter.''

"I can never make out whether you're honest
and true for scouting or not,'' poor Skinny
said.

"Oh, I'm honest and true,'' said Danville.
"Tell me and let's plan it out and get it over
with.''

"You got to be serious about it,'' Skinny
warned.

"All right, I'll start crying if you say so. As
I understand it I've got to hike seven miles
and seven miles back and write up an account
of it—all the time being serious. Now is this
cave just exactly seven miles? I don't want to
make that hike and then find I didn't go far
enough. And if I should find I hiked farther
than necessary I'd be good and mad at you.
I'm not going to give them any more than they
ask for; I'm a stingy chap.''

"Is it a real pony—a live one?" Skinny asked.

"If it isn't I'll have my dad arrested for swindling."

"Would you have anybody arrested?"

"I might if I happened to think of it. Let's talk about something pleasant. If I do that fourteen mile hike and close up on the first class tests, will you find me a boy to train as a tenderfoot? That'll be the only thing left to do. Maybe you could leave the scouts and then I'd start in training you—no?"

"They wouldn't let us do that. Just the same we'll find some feller that's not a scout."

"All right then, I guess I might as well take a hop, skip and jump into the first class. Will you go with me to-morrow morning and hold my hand?"

"Sure I will; then I can tell them I was the one that went with you, hey? I can be the one to prove it."

"Sure thing; you tell 'em."

"Are you all excited about it?" Skinny asked.

"Oh I think I'll sleep to-night."

"And to-morrow you can write to your father that you're a full first class scout, hey?"

"Don't forget about the boy I have to catch and train for a tenderfoot."

"Yes, but that isn't exactly a *test,* kind of."

"Now if you weren't such a little peach of a scout I might use *you.*"

"And I could go in your patrol, maybe; hey? Because my patrol wouldn't be mad if I did."

"Oh, is that so? Well, we'll have to be careful not to make them mad. I suppose they'd beat us up if they got mad; and they wouldn't let us use your canoe."

Skinny seemed to be thinking. "If you're breaking in a new feller then maybe you won't bother with me any more; hey?"

"Then again maybe I will."

"I bet when you get your first class badge, then you'll start getting a lot of merit badges; I bet you'll win a whole lot of them."

"Six or eight at a time, huh?"

"And when you've got your first class badge you can try for camp specials too. Those are things that are not in the Handbook, like the Mohawk Archery set for tracking; you get a target easel and a lot of targets and a real Indian bow and arrows and everything. You've got to track somebody, or an animal, five miles through the woods—then you get it."

"I kind of like that."

"First you've got to find tracks—I'll help you. There's a feller up here named Roy Blakeley; don't you let *him* help you. He told one scout where there were some tracks and they were nothing but railroad tracks. So do you want to try for that prize after you get your full badge?"

"That's the one for me. Tell me about this canoe; how did you win it?"

"I was all kinder crazy like—kinder like my fingers were asleep. So I even couldn't hold myself back. Do you say a feller can be kinder good even if he's reckless. You don't have to be so terrible if you're bad, do you?"

"Guess not."

"If you like me a lot——"

"That's it."

"If you like me a lot and I do something— kinder—maybe—if I'm kind of not so good all of a sudden—then would you like me just the same?"

Danville Bently gazed amusedly at the poor little fellow wedged into the point of the canoe. There was something pathetic about Skinny's very posture as he sat there, serious, eager, insignificant. He looked out of place and uncomfortable in this beautiful canoe, as if he did not yet comprehend how he had even won it.

His own spectacular excursion into the field of heroic enterprise was like a fairy tale to him now. But he was strong on hero worship. Danville lifted the paddle and poked him with it; Skinny was used to that sort of thing.

"No, I only like Sunday School boys," said Danville. "They've got to be perfect to suit me."

Skinny looked at him as if he did not know whether to believe this or not.

"So if you've been committing any murders or robbing any banks, it's all over between us. Shall we flop around toward camp again now, and wash up for eats?"

"To-morrow morning you'll go on Test Four?"

"To-morrow morning. Then for the archery set and the new recruit."

"Can I be partners with you while you're doing all that?"

"Sure—or falling down on it."

"Sometimes fellers forget when they have dates with me."

"Well I've got a good memory."

CHAPTER XXIII

HENNY'S CAVE

Skinny did not quite comprehend this rather whimsical boy. But here was a prize he had every intention of keeping. He no longer worried about Danny. That dreadful affair which had cost him sleepless nights was at last over. Danny had triumphed (if you call it triumph) and gone upon his dubious way. All that remained of that fearful nightmare was Skinny's love and admiration of the checkered hero.

Danny was far away and safe. His genius for beating any game would carry him through every difficulty. There was one place where he would always be safe and that was in the stout little heart that beat beneath the the shabby and faded shirt of his little half brother. There Danny dwelt, but nobody knew it. Only Skinny wished that they would take that dreadful notice from the bulletin-board.

But now he had a new worry. He feared that he would lose this scout of the white scarf, just as he had lost his prize canoe. Because he knew that prize canoes and tall scouts with

white scarfs were not for him. He made no
complaint that his canoe had been absorbed
into his patrol, even if he himself had not been
absorbed into it. He had never quite compre-
hended the glittering romance of his induction
into scouting and that fine patrol.

But he did want to "keep in" with Danville
Bently. And he lived in mortal fear of losing
him, even as he had lived in mortal fear of
Danny's being found out during that awful
fortnight of his presence in camp. He saw that
Danville was admired, that the whole camp was
puzzled at his choice and he feared that any
moment this splendid, picturesque boy would
be lured into the maelstrom and be lost to him.
Particularly he was afraid of the Vermont
Eagle, Howell Cross. What had he, Skinny, to
offer as against the delights of comradeship
with that crack patrol? He slept hardly an
hour that whole night, fearing that something
might happen to ruin his sponsorship of Danville's one remaining test for first class rank.
His high strung nature was all worked up with
fear and expectancy. Again his "hands felt as
if they were asleep kinder, all tingly," the
same as when he had plunged into the lake, and
when he had lifted the white pennant. Because, you see, the whole thing was too good to

HE LED THE WAY, CRAWLING ON HANDS AND KNEES.

Skinny McCord.

be true. That night they "kidded" him at
camp-fire, but he did not mind. He went up to
Elks' cabin and lay restlessly all night, waiting for the morning.

He did not dare to approach Danville at
breakfast where he sat with a group from Tent
Village. But after breakfast he went down to
the lake and there was Danville waiting.
Again his hero of the white scarf had not failed
him.

"I thought maybe I only dreamed it," said
Skinny.

"I guess it will turn out to be a pretty strenuous dream," Danville answered. "Well, are
we all set?"

"Sure, and I got Chocolate Drop to make me
some sandwiches; see? He's a good friend of
mine."

"One cook is better than a dozen scouts;
huh?"

"Sure, but are you going to join Howell
Cross's patrol for the season?"

"Don't you know I've got a patrol of my
own?"

"That's what I can never remember, because
kinder you seem all by yourself, as if there
weren't any fellers like you. Do they all wear
white scarfs and belts like you?"

"Yep. Come on now, for the big parade."

"I'll show you," said Skinny eagerly.

Henny's Cave was an ideal destination for scouts making the fourteen mile hike specified in Test Four. It was exactly seven miles distant through the woods and supplied en route much material for the required written description. An observant scout would not miss the crooked willow tree with the two trunks a few yards east of the path. If his hearing was keen he would find Spook Falls down in the hollow, and note this crystal cascade as one of the things observed. But few were the scouts who saw in the chewed and broken branches at one spot a clue to the location of a beaver dam a quarter of a mile or so off the trail.

The cave itself was an interesting natural phenomenon with a rocky entrance as well concealed as that of any pirate's lair. Inside it was as large as a small room, dank and dark. But if you directed a search-light here and there against its wet, rocky walls you would see scores of names and initials scratched upon the surface to prove that the weary artists had achieved their seven mile hike and might claim credit for Test Four. The verification was usually enough for the presiding powers.

It was nearly noontime when Danville and

Skinny approached this romantic destination
after their long hike over mountains and
through dense woods. "I'm glad I don't have
to write up the account of it with my feet,"
said Danville. "This is some spooky place; I
bet ghosts live here. Let's take a look inside
and then we'll sit out under this tree and eat."

"You have to stoop down and crawl under
that rock," said Skinny, "and then you walk
between those two others; it's really one big
rock that's split; then you're on the inside. In
the middle it's water so you have to step
around the edge, but there's plenty of room
where it's dry. There's lots of little red lizards
inside. If you catch one by the tail it's good
luck."

"Not for the lizard."

"No, for the feller that catches him by the
tail."

"You got a flash-light?" Danville asked.

Of course Skinny had no flash-light; he had
nothing mentioned in the alluring scout equip-
ment list. But he did try to "be prepared" in
his humble way and he had a metal shaving-
stick box containing a few matches. This
gloomy cave was his exhibit and he proudly led
the way, crawling on hands and knees under
the slab of overhanging rock which was a sort

of vestibule leading under an uprooted tree.
Part of this great root (enough to keep the
fallen tree alive) still had anchorage in the
ground, but the sun-baked tentacles of the
rest of it hung in air like some outlandish
whip-lash curtain and through this mass the
visitor must crawl, assailed by these lifeless,
dangling pendants. This grotesque approach
opened upon a cleft between great rocks, or
the parted halves of one great rock, and here
the explorer could walk erect through a passage roofed by the great tree that had fallen
over the top of the cleft. It was an intricate
entrance to the dank, secluded chamber within,
an earthly and rocky dungeon where one's
voice sounded strange to one's own ears.

Probably the disturbance caused by the
breaking apart of that great rock had forced
open this tiny apartment in the dense hillside,
who shall say how many years ago? Nor did
any one know who Henny was, whose name was
perpetuated in this gloomy retreat. There was
a legend that he had lived on a farm and had
been buried alive here in a quick transforma-
tion of the uncertain walls. Enterprising
scouts had searched for his bones, but there
seemed to be nothing left of the unknown Henny
save only his name. Of course, the place was

one of Captain Kidd's many safe deposit vaults, but no vestige of his fabulous treasure was ever found by Temple Camp excavators.

"Great Scott!" said Danville as he looked about in the darkness, and gropingly felt for the dank walls. "Gives you the shudders; I feel as if I were buried alive. Where are you anyway?"

"Here I am," said Skinny, delighted at Danville's reaction to the place. "Look out where you step, there's all water. The ground slants up in one place and it's dry there. Wait till I light a match."

To Danville the feeling of confinement in this gruesome hole was all but unnerving. It needed only the warning that it was not safe to move in the darkness to give him the feeling that he was indeed buried alive in this ghostly, stifling place. One little glint of uncertain light he did see, cheerful reminder of the bright world without, and this was the only beacon to show where the intricate entrance was. It was a mere speck of light leaking through under those weird tree roots and through the rocky passage.

"Wait till I strike a match," said Skinny.

"Hsh, listen!" whispered Danville. "Did you hear a sound?"

"No, you always kind of hear noises in here," said Skinny.

"No, but I heard something moving. I thought it was you, but you're on the other side of me. Hurry up, your matches won't last anyway. I wish we had a candle or something."

Just as he said this there was a slight rustling near him like the sound of paper being crumpled. He knew that Skinny had no paper.

CHAPTER XXIV

MISSING

The startling thing that followed, happened suddenly. Skinny struck a match and in its brief uncertain light Danville saw him stumble and fall. For just a second he was aware of something that looked like a log and he supposed that Skinny had tripped on this. Then he sniffed smoke and in less than half a minute the tiny place was full of suffocating fumes. Yet there was no blaze, only a little red glow which shed no illumination.

"Quick, get out of here," Danville gasped. "See that little streak of daylight? Follow that, it's the entrance."

"I know, you come too," Skinny said, as he began coughing.

"Get down and crawl," Danville was just able to say; "keep near the ground!" He was overcome by a paroxysm of coughing but he heard, half-consciously, a sound which he thought to be Skinny crawling away. "All right?" he asked, his senses reeling. He heard Skinny answer, but the words were not clear.

167

He did not know whether that was because Skinny could not speak clearly or because of the drumming in his own ears. His eyes were streaming and he fought for every breath.

He would have fallen unconscious if he had not lowered himself to a crawling posture. Even so the ground seemed uncertain under him, like a yielding mattress. But he was in muddy water and the wetness reminded him to pull off his scarf and saturate it in the puddle. Hardly conscious of what he did, he pulled the dripping scarf over his head and face, gathering up the end of it between his teeth.

His head swam, his hands trembled, but with his face swathed in the dripping scarf he was measurably restored. He was conscious of the gritty taste of thin mud in his mouth, and the stinging in his eyes diminished. For a few seconds he was sufficiently master of his senses to wish that he had reminded Skinny to wet his shirt and take it in his teeth. He called but the word he uttered did not sound like Skinny to his swimming brain.

He was just conscious enough to know that he must act quickly. His improvised mask afforded but incomplete and temporary relief, and he knew that he was tottering on the brink of oblivion. But by pulling the scarf away from his eyes he was able to see that little glint which told of the fresh air and the bright, clear world outside. On hands and knees he crawled toward it. Suddenly his hand lay against something soft; he felt cloth, then hair, then a face. His senses were reeling now, his head bursting. He gathered more of the wet scarf into his mouth. In a vague way he realized that this soft object was Skinny, that the little fellow had not escaped, but had sunk unconscious.

He could not speak to ask a question. What he did he seemed to be doing in a trance. But he got his arm around the prostrate form and hauled it with him toward the tiny beacon. To his ebbing senses the fume-filled place seemed vast, he was oddly persuaded that he had miles of suffocating area to cross, hauling his limp burden. Even the little glint of light deserted him. It did not disappear, but there were other lights, not real, but in his reeling brain. They came and went like stars and he knew not which light to follow.

Still he moved, slowly, uncertainly; one might say unconsciously. He fell over his lifeless burden, let his throbbing head rest for just a moment on the soft body, then gathered

the wet scarf again into his mouth and knew
that he was still alive by the gritty, earthy
taste in his mouth. He could not keep his
stinging eyes open, but he thought, or rather
felt (for his mind was not capable of thinking)
that he was near the entrance. Instinctively he
reached out a clammy hand and groped for the
light, as if it were something tangible that he
could get hold of. His cold, trembling fingers closed upon a bit of root in the rocky passage. The knowledge of this inner entrance had
quite passed from his mind, but instinctively he
clutched the root and pulled with all his might,
dragging the body after him. He knew (as one
is conscious in a dream) that he was pulling
with one hand, dragging something with the
other, and helping his progress with both feet,
in this final, supreme, spasmodic effort.

And it brought him to where the air was a
little clearer. Even here in the passage it was
thick and stifling, but it was mixed with the
pure air of heaven. He never knew how he
groped his way out. But there came a moment
when he pushed the muddy, drenched scarf
from his mouth and breathed freely, though his
head pounded and his eyes stung. He was
under the tilted root of the great tree, brushing the dangling tentacles aside with his hand

as he crawled through, dragging his burden after him. Not until he emerged on the rugged, green hillside did he pause. He heard a bird singing. Just as he sank back in utter exhaustion he saw several crows in flight overhead; their cawing sounded miles away. Idly, half-consciously, he tried to count them.

Hazily, he looked at the face of the boy he had dragged to safety. It was streaked with blood and dirt from contact with the rocky earth. The eyes were closed; the body lay limp, in a way to strike terror, with an arm extended as if the prostrate thing were making a speech. The victim wore a scout suit which was in shreds and covered with mud. Danville blinked his stinging eyes, trying with his slowly returning senses to comprehend this strange sequel to his harrowing adventure. He did not know what to make of it; all that he knew was that the boy was not Skinny.

And Skinny was nowhere to be seen.

CHAPTER XXV

FROM ABOVE

At the moment when Skinny had crawled out of the cave an inspiration had come to him. He had no idea what had caused the suffocating fumes which had filled the place. The cave, as he remembered it, contained nothing inflammable into which his lighted match could have fallen; nor anything on which he could have tripped. Yet he had stumbled on something of considerable bulk. However, he did not pause to consider these mysteries.

He emerged into the fresh air and daylight, coughing incessantly. He called to make sure that Danville was following, but there was no answer. Astonished and concerned, he re-approached the entrance, calling. Not hearing any answer he was seized with panic fear. To reënter the cave was quite impossible. Even the outer entrance under the tree root was smoky, and the passage between the rocks was filled with the dense fumes. That was at about the moment when Danville thought to soak his scarf in the muddy water. Skinny shouted into the volume of emerging smoke, but it stifled him, even where he stood in the open, and he was compelled to withdraw from the entrance.

It was then he had his inspiration. He remembered that very early that summer he and Charlie Avery, a new boy from Long Island, had seen a little speck of light in the low roof of the cave. Charlie had poked his scout staff up through this and Skinny had gone out and scrambled up to see if it had penetrated through to the open air. He found that it had, and that by reason of a rather odd condition. This cave was part of a jumble of dense brush and fallen trees; it had probably been made in some terrific storm. A tree on the hillock above the cave had been blown over, doubtless from the same cause which had uprooted the one below that formed part of the intricate entrance. Indeed the spot was a tangled jungle of rock and dense brush and fallen trees, and the cave only a grotto caused by the upheaval.

In falling, this tree above the cave had wrenched part of its root up and it was just in this depression, now soggy and overgrown, that Charlie Avery's staff had gone through. If the little dungeon underneath had been lighted one could have seen the disturbance caused by that

wrenching from above, and it was one of the
standard jokes of Temple Camp to tell a new
boy there were snakes in the cave and then
direct his groping progress against a dangling
end of root that hung down into the dank,
earthy vault. The startled visitor usually re-
acted very satisfactorily to this. Here, you will
understand, the roof of the cave was thinnest,
and the ground in the excavation where the
root had been was soft because of the water
that was continually collecting in it and seep-
ing through into the cave. Some day there
would be a cave-in here, but no one ever worried about it.

Skinny knew about all this and now it occurred to him that he might work open a hole
in this soft depression and release the fumes
more rapidly than they would escape through
the entrance. It was, indeed, the only rescue
work that he could do. He was already fearful
that it would be too late to save his friend. If
his effort resulted in a cave-in, even so that
would release the smoke and probably not completely engulf the victim.

Breaking off a branch from a tree, he began
churning it around in the soft earth with fever-
ish excitement. He became possessed, just as
when he had won the prize canoe. His emo-

tional power (which no one knew about) gave him strength, and he strove with maniacal effort to get the stick down, pushing it, then working it in a circle. Soon it broke and he secured another, so large that he could hardly handle it. When it became blocked by rock or bits of root he actually cried in nervous excitement and gave vent to his annoyance by screaming. One cannot keep this sort of thing up very long; the nerves give out if the strength does not. Skinny was on the verge of hysteria. But still he strove like a little David with his great unwieldy Goliath of a stick, pushing, twisting, pulling, crying, falling and rising again, and hanging on it to pry open a hole into that stifling tomb below.

At last something happened. The stick plunged, Skinny lost his balance and went sprawling into the depression. But he smelled smoke. He had been successful, the long stick had penetrated into the cave. Right beside him a thin column rose and dissolved in the air. He rose, breathing excitedly, and holding a cut knee. But he did not care. He grabbed hold of the stick again, pulling the end of it around in a large circle to enlarge the tiny hole he had made. He tripped, he stumbled, and again cut himself sorely when he went sprawling on a

bit of pointed rock. But he was up again, pulling, hauling, wrenching. He was in a state of
frenzy, this insignificant, staring little fellow
whom they "jollied." He seemed to be fight-
ing the whole universe, wrestling with the
elements. Blood was streaming from his cut
leg, his face was dripping with sweat, his eyes
were wild.

Suddenly the ground on which he stood settled, he heard a dim thud, and the stick descended till only a few inches of it remained
above surface. Now the smoke came out
freely; there was no cave-in, but something had
happened. In his small way, Skinny had
changed the face of nature. Frantic with joy
he brushed the smoke away from his face and
tried to haul the stick up. Then he saw something which he could hardly believe; it seemed
like magic, and to conjure his whole maniacal
striving into a tumultuous dream. As he
raised the long stick a snake was coiled loosely
about it.

Slowly, almost mechanically the drowsy reptile included Skinny's leg in its slow winding.
It tightened around the stick and the little thin
limb binding them together like things bound
around with cord. The action of the snake was
not belligerent, it seemed asleep and made the

horrible affair seem unreal. Its movement was like the weirdly slow motion pictures sometimes shown so as to reveal detail to the spectators. There was something appalling in its slow, drowsy tightening.

CHAPTER XXVI

WITH THE SMOKE

Dreamy, that was the way it seemed to the panic-stricken Skinny. The thing was so unreal! Following immediately upon his frantic striving, this loathsome thing had slowly emerged upon the stick and by a kind of sluggish inevitable instinct incorporated Skinny's thin leg in its unconscious coiling. There he was bound by this living horror to the big limb he had been using.

So drowsily deliberate was the long snake that it would have seemed not amiss to remind it of its ghastly error. But if its instinctive action had been purposeless it was none the less effectual. It was tightly coiled around these two dissimilar supports; it seemed as free of malice and intention as so much binding rope. But even in his astonishment and fright, Skinny saw that it was a great rattlesnake; its bony appendage looked like a pine cone lying against the branch. Bound to this branch as he was, he could not stand and he sank down exhausted and terror-stricken in the depression. It was the usual sort of climax to his heroic achievements.

He was in no condition to ponder on the cause of this singular happening, but the reader will surmise the facts. The snake was probably in a stupor caused by the fumes below when Skinny's long implement descended into the suffocating cave. Instinctively it had coiled itself about the stick and was lifted out before its coiling was complete. The depth of its stupor may be conceived by its drowsy action of including the adjacent leg of its rescuer as it settled into coiled inertness.

If Skinny could have stood erect perhaps he would have had some command of himself, would have thought of something to do. But he was at the same disadvantage as a person is who has been knocked down. He was powerless till he could rise; and he could not rise. His whole little trembling body seemed involved in this ghastly attack. If he had been bound and thrown into that little muddy jungle, he would have felt less fearful, less at the mercy of a foe. But this horrifying thing had occurred without a struggle on his part. He had striven like one possessed, till his stout little heart beat like a trip-hammer, and then, in the proud moment of his triumph this deadly

reptile had slowly, silently, probably unconsciously coiled its slimy, clinging form around
his leg, and he had gone down in defeat—perhaps to death.

But he got hold of his senses. Should he
dare to call? If Danville was alive and conscious, he would hear and perhaps rescue him.
But how? What could Danville do that he,
Skinny, could not do? Anything that either of
them tried to do would be perilous, might precipitate a fatal sequel. If he moved or shouted,
he might arouse the torpid thing whose clammy
coldness he could feel against his torn stocking.
His leg was not bound for its whole length, but
he dared not even wriggle his foot. The reptile was so tightly coiled that the circulation
was embarrassed in his leg and his foot was
asleep. Yet he dared not seek relief by moving it about. His predicament was appalling,
unnerving, especially to a boy of his highly
strung nature.

He tried to bring himself to scream. That
might either bring help or death. Quick help
or quick death. But probably Danville was already dead. The smoke was pouring out like
smoke out of a chimney; it was a good job this
little mascot had done. Why did not Danville
shout, or appear? Surely, if he was safe, he

would not fail to see the smoke rising from the jungly hillock; he would scramble up and investigate. The thought of the smoke caused him to indulge the hope that this mounting column he had released might be seen at camp; that if he just lay motionless perhaps some one would come and rescue him from this grotesque predicament. But in his heart he knew that it would not be seen at camp, seven miles distant.

The smoke was thinning out now and loathsome little bugs with many legs crawled rapidly about, seeking their wonted shelter under damp logs; they were part of the exodus from that stifling inferno, hardier than humans in their battle with the deadly fumes. One of them crawled aimlessly across Skinny's face, but he dared not move his arm to brush it away. He saw one of his familiar little red lizards making its way up the stick and across the rattlesnake as if it did not mind this poisonous reptile in the least.

Suddenly a thought came which startled him. This loathsome snake would come out of its stupor now that it was in the pure, clear air. It would realize where it was and would sting him. It would sting him right where its horrible head lay, a little above his knee. He strained his eyes, pressed his chin into his chest, and looked at that frightful head. The little beady eyes were open; it was hard to believe that the snake was stupefied. But at least it did not shoot out its cruel, darting tongue. It remained quite motionless. It seemed satisfied if he was. But why should it remain long inert when these escaping denizens of the cave were able to make good their rush to safety?

Skinny knew that his only chance lay in prompt action; that when the snake began to move, it would not release itself and crawl away. It would bite him and he would die in an hour. That was what Uncle Jeb Rushmore had said, about an hour *"more ner less."* Well, he was too wrought up to lie there waiting for death; he must do something. The thought occurred to him that if he had a jack-knife, he could stab the snake. But you see he had no jack-knife, he had nothing that scouts have. So he resolved to shout. Perhaps Danville was alive and would hear him. And perhaps his voice would not arouse the drowsy reptile to bite him. If it did and Danville came, then Danville would know what had happened. He believed that if Danville had not been stifled to death, he would be emerging into consciousness by now.

By rolling over just a little bit he might be able to look down into the opening he had made. He had not directly made that opening; that is, he had not worked it all out with his stick. He thought he must have dislodged a stone that had fallen into the cave, and thus broken the root-bound earth. Suppose he looked down into that dark inferno—suppose there was light there. Something, he knew not what, had caught fire there. And suppose the rock he had dislodged had fallen on Danville lying prostrate and overcome. . . .

Skinny had too much imagination. Well, he must not imagine things now, but act. He made up his mind what he would do. He would shout. That, of course, would agitate his body and probably arouse his torpid foe to deadly action. If that occurred he would quickly wrench his tattered shirt off, pull it around his skinny little leg, and tie it in a knot. Then he would reach for a stick which he saw, slip it under the encircling shirt and turn it, drawing the shirt tighter and tighter around his wounded limb just above the point of the deadly bite. He thought that the bite would be just about where the head was, on the front of his leg just above the knee. He had the stick all picked out. Suddenly the wild thought came to him of reaching down and grabbing the serpent by the neck. But he was so placed with relation to it that he could not apply the necessary strength. Shouting was best, at least as a first recourse.

So he shouted.

CHAPTER XXVII

SKINNY'S HERO

Danville Bently was not fifty feet distant from Skinny. He was bending over the boy he had rescued and was just recovering from his consternation at finding him a stranger when he heard the shouting. It was rather odd that Skinny's frantic call caused this prostrate boy to open his eyes, by which Danville knew that he still lived. He closed them again, as if he had been disturbed in slumber.

Danville scrambled up through tangled brush to the summit of the overgrown mound which enclosed the cave. Smoke was still coming from the hole; the place looked like a miniature volcano in the crater of which lay Skinny, the long branch which he had used tight against him like a stilt.

"Don't—don't touch me," he breathed almost in anguish; "keep away—look—the snake."

Danville could hardly believe his eyes. "He bit you?" he asked quickly.

"No he didn't—he's sort of asleep or something—don't scare him—he came out where I
made a hole so—so as to save you. He's dopy
from the smoke, I guess."

"He's not so dopy," said Danville, as the
reptile shot out his tongue; "he's awake enough
to do that. Lie still, that isn't what he bites
you with; don't get excited. I wish I had my
scarf if we need a twister." *

For a moment he paused, thinking and glancing about. Skinny lay trembling, not daring
to stir. Somehow he was more fearful and
excited than he had been before his friend's
arrival; something was to be done and it might
precipitate a fatal sequel. "Anyway *you* got
safe," he said.

"Keep still—I know—now just, just a second," Danville said.

He moved with lightning stealth now.
Quickly he took out his jack-knife, opened it,
and held it between his teeth while he hurried
to the nearest tree and pulled off a large piece
of bark which was already warping away from
the dried trunk. This was perhaps a foot in
diameter. He next pulled off his shirt, tore a
strip from it and looking about picked up a

* Meaning a tourniquet, or bandage drawn tight by turning
an inserted stick.

stick suitable for his purpose. Thus completely prepared he stole up, motioning Skinny to lie still, and laid the stick and the torn strip of shirt on the ground within easy reach. Then with lightning dexterity he slipped the piece of bark downward along Skinny's leg till it was stopped by the snake's coiled body. But it lay between that cruel head and Skinny's flesh, and being rounded to the curve of the tree, it fitted rather nicely.

With another movement that can only be described as instantaneous, he plunged his jack-knife into the drowsy reptile's head. He was none too quick, for even as he did so its horrid tongue was darting, and scarcely had the knife touched its scaly head when its fangs were plunged against the bark. But there ended its deadly power; it was pinned to the protecting bark, and a trickle of blood flowed from Skinny's leg where the knife had pierced through. There was a spasmodic tightening of the coils around his little limb, then a loosening bringing infinite relief.

"Did he bite me?" Skinny asked pitifully.

"No, he's gone out of that business," said Danville, lifting Skinny's big implement of rescue with the snake hanging limply over it. "See? Look at the size of him, will you! That

was a blamed funny thing to happen, hey? He
got busy just too late."

"Don't—don't drop him near me," Skinny
pleaded, as his rescuer dangled the loathsome
body. "My leg stings, I think he bit me."

"No he didn't, Alf; I just jabbed you with
my knife. Look." He held up the curving slab
of bark and there upon it was a tiny wet spot,
appalling evidence of the deadly substance that
had been ejected from those deadly fangs.
"He struck out, but it was meant for a home
run all right," Danville said. "Come on, don't
be scared, come down and see my new boy
friend. I'm going to pass you up now, I've got
a new pal."

Skinny did get up at that. "See where I
made a hole?" he said. "All the smoke came
out here and maybe it saved you, hey?"

"I think I must have been out when you
started, Alf. I pulled somebody out, I thought
it was you; I guess I came blamed near getting
suffocated. I don't know how I got out, all I
know is I got out. I guess some scout from
camp must have hiked here ahead of us; he's
still dopy. What the dickens happened anyway? There wasn't anything that would burn
in that damp place, was there?"

"Whatever it was, it was damp," said

Skinny; "that's what made the smoke so thick; it was smudge smoke, like what scouts use for signals. Even little bugs came out. I lit a match and then I stumbled over something that was never there before. Anyway, one thing sure, you'll get the Gold Cross. You'll get it for saving me, and you'll get it for saving that other feller. I bet I know who it is, too; it's Pompy Arliss in that Brooklyn troop, because he's out for Test Four, and I was telling him about the cave. But I didn't know he was on his test to-day. You know the feller I mean, that wears his hair all sticking up? He's all the time kidding me."

They scrambled down, working their way through the thick underbrush and over rocks, making slow progress because of Skinny's bleeding leg, which soon they had to bandage effectively before going on.

"And how about you?" Danville asked.

"As long as I know I didn't get bit by poison," Skinny said in his quaint way; "as long as I know that I don't care."

"I mean about the Gold Cross," Danville said. "Is that bandage too tight—no? I mean about what *you* did."

"I didn't save anybody, I only tried to," said Skinny. "You don't get it for only try-

ing. But maybe if you were still in there I'd
have saved you, hey? But you get it twice,
kinder. And I'm just as glad, too, because now
I got a friend that's a hero. So are you going
to stay my friend even now? Even when you
get the Gold Cross, are you? I won't be mad
if you don't—but are you? Because now Howell Cross and all those scouts will *surely* be after
you! Because the Gold Cross is the biggest,
specialest thing in scouting. Even it's greater
than being an Eagle—even. It's for saving life
when you risk your own, like you did—*twice
even.* Because that snake might have killed
you, mightn't he? So now you'll get your first
class badge, and you'll get the Gold Cross, and
will you let me be the first one to see it? I bet
you're proud, hey—that you'll get it? Do you
know who'll give it to you? Not anybody that
belongs at camp—not trustees even. A commissioner! A national one!"

"No!"

"Honest, I cross my heart. So will you go
around with me kinder steady, even after
that?"

"No, that's asking too much," Danville
laughed.

"I can tell you're joking."

For answer Danville only drew the little,

limping fellow close to him, and so they picked
their way down through the brambly thicket off
the eminence which enclosed the little cave.

"Sure I'm proud, Alf," laughed Danville
frankly.

"Then why don't you act so?"

"Do you want me to dance a jig in this jungle?"

"You'll be the big hero of Temple Camp,
that's what you'll be. Even they print all
about you in the newspapers, when you get the
Gold Cross."

"And do you think I'm going to forget all
about the pal that was with me when I won it?"
Danville asked, rather more earnestly than was
his wont.

"Because," said Skinny with that nervous
eagerness that Temple Camp was so fond of
mimicking, "now I got a friend that's a hero
and I can talk about him. Because my brother
Danny, I couldn't talk about him to fellers, but
I can talk about you all I want—how you're a
hero."

"Take your time, I haven't got it yet," said
Danville.

"Sure, you've as much as got it."

"Don't count your chickens till they're
hatched. When I get it I'll have it."

They picked their way down by a circuitous route and around to the entrance of the cave where Danville's rescued victim of the fumes sat on the ground with hands clasped around his updrawn knees, blinking and looking about in a dazed kind of way. Skinny stopped short, his whole thin little body trembling.

"Danny!" he cried. "It's Danny, it's my brother! It's Danny that you pulled out of the cave! Danny, nobody knows where you are, and they didn't catch you, hey? The reform school people—Danny?"

"Who's the guy you've got with you?" Danny asked uneasily.

HE PLUNGED HIS JACK-KNIFE INTO THE REPTILE'S HEAD.

Skinny Mc Cord. *Page* 189

CHAPTER XXVIII

There was no chance of escape now. The simplicity and trustfulness of Skinny's nature supervened and there, in the very presence of his wretched half-brother, he told about the whole miserable affair of Danny's masquerade at camp. Danville Bently, greatly astonished, sat on a rock listening. He did not seem to be angry, his face was a puzzle. He had picked up his dripping, muddy scarf and held it dangling in the final pause when the two half-brothers had ceased speaking. While still they talked he had glanced rather curiously from one to the other, paying to each the tribute of friendly attention. And now, when he spoke, his casual remark bore no reference to Skinny's concealment, to Danny's fraud, or to his dubious record.

"You'd never guess that scarf used to be white, would you?" he asked, looking at neither Skinny nor Danny. "That was white silk. Lucky I've got a couple more of them." Then after a pause, "I'll bet you found it pretty

193

damp in that blamed rat-hole. What did you haul the log in there for?"

"So as to keep the leaves from spreading," Danny said. "I carried them in and piled them between the log and the wall."

"Some bed," said Danville. "You must have got good and tired of eating fish. How'd you do, fry them?"

"Yep, that's easy."

"And that what's-his-name you took the blame for—Sharpe? He just let it go at that, huh?"

"I don't take any credit," Danny said. "I'd have been found out when you showed up anyway. Sharpy's nothing but a flivver; let him have his fun."

"Look how I can wring the water out of this darned thing," Danville said. "Lucky there was water in the cave, hey? I wish you could go back to camp with us. It's a sticker, what we're going to do now. We all came through with our lives fine and dandy, and now we don't know what to do."

"You're not mad at him?" Skinny asked.

"I never get mad," said Danville. "Only I don't see how he's going to go back to camp— I'm kind of mad about that. We could have some fun."

"Oh I'll go back," said Danny, desperately. "I'm out of luck; what's the use trying to beat the game? You did the kid a good turn, and you did me one too; you saved the both of us. I've got the camp after me at one end and the school bunch after me at the other—I'm through. Come on, we'll go back and you can get your Gold Cross, we'll take care of that, won't we, Tiny? What do you think we are— half-baked sports? Just because I pulled a slope * on the reformatory? Hey, Tiny, tell him how I smashed Kinney, and that boy scout for what he said."

"I did tell him, he knows," said Skinny.

"Sure, I'll go back; all they can do is give me over to that bunch of dopes at Blythedale and I'll get a couple of years extra, if I don't pull another slope on them. They sleep standing up, that menagerie of yaps. What I did for Sharpy, the boy detective, I can do for you. I may be black, but I ain't yellow."

"What color would you say I am—not counting the mud on me?" said Danville. "I never said I wanted any Gold Cross. I saved Alf because he's my side partner. And as long as I saved *you* I might as well finish the job. I'm

* The elegant phrase meaning *escaped*.

not going to say I came to this place at all;
I'm not going to say I saved either one of you.
And I'm not going to make a strike for the
badge on this hike. It's all off. If I say I saved
Alf then there'll be a whole lot of questions,
and nix on lying. Nobody knows we came here
and nobody needs to know it. I've got twenty
dollars and I'll give it to you—ten for smash-
ing Kinney, and ten for that other fellow for
what he said. Will you look at the mud on that
twenty spot? It went right through my clothes.
You visited me for two weeks in camp only I
didn't know it, and my dad will pay the bill.
Why don't you go back to reform school?"

"Would you?" Danny asked.

"Hanged if I know; only won't they get
you?"

"Not if I can once get on a ship."

"Well, you have to mind your business, and I
have to mind mine. And maybe I can't see my
way clear to go by notices on bulletin boards.
Anyway, I forgot all about saving anybody's
life and making the fourteen mile hike, and
you're a darned good scout only you don't
know it. I'd rather be you than Sharpy. I
came up here to have a good time and not to be
a detective. I don't care a hang about the Gold
Cross. You can't prove anything by me."

"You mean you're not going to tell—how you found him, and how you saved us both?" Skinny asked excitedly. "You mean you're not going to get the *Gold Cross?*"

Danville Bently shook his head and made a wry face. "I don't like it, it costs too much," said he. "I'm a stingy scout and I won't pay the price. Come on, what do you say we eat? Tea for three. How the dickens can you cut two sandwiches to make three helpings? There's a sticker. Got a lead pencil and I'll see if I can do it by geometry."

CHAPTER XXIX

Thus ended the adventures of Danny Mc-
Cord in the neighborhood of Temple Camp.
He had been an expensive luxury during his
brief and colorful sojourn. He had cost poor
Skinny much worry, and he had cost Danville
Bently the Gold Cross for heroism. He went
forth upon his way with Skinny's scout suit
(much the worse for wear) and the twenty dollars that Danville had insisted on his taking.
His unexpired term at reform school must also
be charged against his account.

Yet I like Danny, even though I do not ap-
prove of him. The blow he struck the historic
Kinney, as also the blow he struck Vic Norris,
was rather to his credit; he was a pretty good
big brother, even if he was not such a very
good boy. And the blow that he did *not* strike
Ralph Warner showed him capable of sacrifice. It was because of this sacrifice that Holman Sharpe remained at Temple Camp and
filled three note books before the season was
over.

We shall meet Danny again in a future story and you are warned not to expect to find angelic wings sprouting on his pugilistic shoulders. He had, I think, the raw material of a scout, but it was very, very raw. He should not be dismissed, however, without mention of an incident which recalled him to Danville Bently after the lone Polar Bear had returned to his beautiful home in Florida. It was in November that Danville received an envelope enclosing ten dollars and a slip of brown wrapping paper on which was scrawled, "Here's a ten spot, see you later about the rest. Danny." The envelope was postmarked Porto Rico, so it seemed likely that Danny had succeeded in ingratiating himself with the captain of some ship or other. He must have made a rather interesting cabin boy.

On their way back to camp, Danville made no mention of Danny and he closed the Gold Cross matter with a few words that his little worshipper, Skinny, had cause to remember. "What's the use talking about it?" said he. "If I won it, I won it. Only nobody knows it. And nobody's going to know it. The Gold Cross is only kind of like a receipt and I don't need any receipt."

"It's people knowing that counts," said Skinny.

"What they don't know won't hurt them," said Danville.

On reaching camp they parted, Danville going to Tent Village to wash up. When Skinny next saw him, he wore another scout suit, and a new white scarf, its wavy and spotless folds falling loosely below where it was gathered into the silver ring, which took the place of the usual scout knot. You would never have supposed he had saved two lives and almost lost his own. And lost the Gold Cross for heroism. His easygoing self-possession was the most conspicuous thing about him; that and the snowy scarf which was the badge of the distant Polar Bear Patrol. Skinny thought he must be a "specially rich feller." And so he was, indeed, with a richness that only generations of gentle breeding can impart.

As for Skinny, he was pretty dirty and he shuffled up to Martha Norris Memorial Cabins in fear and trembling lest his sorry appearance and sore knee cause embarrassing questions. But no questions were asked, perhaps because Skinny always had a sorry look. "Playing in the mud?" was all that Vic Norris asked of this little fellow who had opened an outlet for the deadly fumes in Henny's Cave. "Must have been tracking mud-turtles," said Hunt Ward. And that was all that any of them said on the dangerous topic of Skinny's adventures.

Perhaps this was because they had something else to say to him. They had something to ask him, and they asked it in ever so nice a way, so that their questions furnished the answer. Connie Bennett, the Elk leader, had told them to leave it to him, that he would "fix it." And he did fix it. He knew just how to handle Skinny.

"Hey kid," said he, "listen. I want to ask you something."

Skinny was not accustomed to be consulted and he gazed at Connie with pleased and eager eyes.

"Listen kid, do you like it in Tent Village?"

"I only go there because Danville Bently is there," said Skinny.

"Sure, and I bet you have a lot of fun there too. Now listen, Shorty; you know Holly Hollis back in Bridgeboro—lives up near where Blakeley lives, on the hill?"

Skinny did not know; he knew nothing about the grand upper world of Bridgeboro. He had once pushed his ramshackle little wagon up to

Terrace Avenue with a clothes basket full of washing for one of the gorgeous houses up there. But Holly Hollis he did not know. He listened, wide-eyed, to this boy who was paying him the compliment of conferring with him.

"I'll tell you how it is, kid. You know the other Bridgeboro Troop that busted up; the one they had in the brick church?"

Skinny did not know, but he listened.

"Well, anyway," said Connie, "they busted up; couldn't get a scoutmaster, I guess. You know Holly, that—he's a sort of a slim fellow? Sure you do! Well, he's an Eagle Scout and he wants to come up here."

"I don't think there's any room in Tent Village, or in Pioneer Row either," said Skinny innocently.

"Sure there isn't, not for a new scout. This is the middle of the season. So we were thinking—now listen. We were thinking if you wanted to stay over there in Tent Village with Bently, they'd put up a cot for you—we'll fix that. Then we could do a good turn to Holly Hollis and let him come up here and bunk in with us, as long as you're having so much fun. And I'll say that Bently's one fine scout all right. Hey, Vic?"

"Sure thing," said Vic Norris.

"You're a lucky kid," said Bert McAlpin.

"Every scout in camp is after that guy," said Stut Moran.

"I'd like to be you all right," said Connie. "Only trouble with him is he's so darned hard to get in with; you never know how to take him. But jiminies, you seem to have him buffaloed, you little rascal."

Skinny smiled, elated, and his wonderful, eager eyes were full of pleasure and pride.

"How do you do it, anyway?" Vic Norris asked.

"Do you mean I won't be a member any more?" Skinny asked.

"Well—no, not exactly that, as you might say," said Connie, as he motioned to the others to let him do the fixing. "You wouldn't say exactly that. But if we form two troops when we get home in the fall, like Mr. Ellsworth says, jiminies, why you'll have your pick of patrols, won't you?"

"Y—yes," said Skinny doubtfully.

"Why sure, why won't you? I'll see to it you stay in our troop if you want. I'm only talking about now, up here at camp. Gee, I thought you were so strong for doing good turns; didn't you, Vic?"

"I sure did," said Vic Norris.

"Skinny's all right, he's one little peach of a scout," said Stut Moran. He did not explain why they did not cling to such a little peach of a scout.

"Why, look at the camps at Bear Mountain," Connie argued. "They bust up troops and patrols just like with dynamite up there. It's all like big families in a lot of those camps. Then when they go home they get together again. You're having a dickens of a good time over there in Tent Village. Where Bently is, that would be good enough for me. *Jiminy crinkums,* I don't know how you got next to that fellow, kid. White Scarf, that's what everybody's calling him."

Skinny was proud, elated, to hear these comments on his hero. He was too guileless to see that what these Elks wanted was an Eagle Scout. He honestly believed, in his stout little heart, that they were keen for a grand good turn. Moreover he did not aspire, he did not dare, to confer on equal terms with these colleagues of his. Yet some little quiver of pride caused him to say:

"It isn't like as if I was expelled is it—so people will think you threw me out?"

"*Threw you out?*" gasped Vic. "Say, how do you get that way? Let any scout say that in my presence—just let me hear him. *Threw you out*—good night! No, but we thought you'd like the idea. We thought we were giving you a big chance. Can't you see it?"

"Y—yes," said Skinny.

"And you'll be up here all the time, won't you?"

"Yes, if you want me to."

"*Want him to*, did you hear that?" said Connie.

Skinny's simple honesty caused them some embarrassment. They were doing this thing artistically, lulling their own consciences, and loading their act onto the back of that willing beast of burden, the good turn. They did not expect anything quite so logical and pathetic as what Skinny now did. He pulled up from under his torn white shirt a piece of string that hung round his neck, detached his locker key from it and handed it to Connie. He was quite too guileless to do this for effect, but it was a little masterpiece and it made Connie feel mean. He was jarred by this perfectly honest response to all he had been saying.

"Oh, you needn't give us that," he said with brusque good-humor. "You're not exactly what you might say getting out."

"Holly Hollis will have to have a locker,"

said Skinny. "Anyway, I haven't got anything in it much."

It is rather to the credit of Bert McAlpin that he turned away, rather ashamed, and pretended to be busy as Connie hesitatingly accepted the key.

The deed was done. It was not as good a piece of work as Skinny had done that day. But of course, nobody knew about that.

CHAPTER XXX

FIXED

Skinny did not understand, but Danville Bently did. Still the little outcast Elk had a certain feeling of humiliation. He knew he had not been "let out," but it might look that way, and he was afraid that Danville would think so. What Danville really did think, Skinny never knew.

But the diplomatic Elks knew, for Danville told them that very evening. Having attended to certain other matters which pleasantly evidenced the esteem in which he was held by the management, he strolled up to Martha Norris Memorial Cabins just before supper, a time when he thought the Elks would be at their patrol cabin.

It was characteristic of Danville that he seemed never to take particular notice of things that were unusually costly and attractive. Perhaps this was because he had been brought up in refined luxury. In any event he seemed always quite at home. He was one of the very few boys at camp who could enter Administra-

tion Shack with perfect ease and speak famil-
iarly to the trustees and councilors. So he did
not take particular note of the three beautiful
large cabins which housed the First Bridgeboro
Troop. He did not even notice the big radio set
in the Elks cabin as he stepped inside, greeting
the scouts who were hurriedly brushing up for
supper. He was thinking of Skinny and not
the realm from which Skinny had been so
neatly ousted.

"I wonder if you fellows want to give me
the key to the boat-locker where Alf keeps his
canoe?" he asked in his easy-going way.
"Seems he forgot to ask you."

If it had been some one else they would probably have challenged his right to come on such
an errand, but there was something about Danville which made them all feel a trifle ill at ease.
There was a certain atmosphere about White
Scarf, as they called him, which caused them to
respect him.

"There's only one key," Connie said.

"Yes, that's the one he wants," said Danville.

"How are *we* going to get in the locker
then?" Vic Norris asked. "That canoe is patrol property; that's a rule in our troop about
prizes."

"Tent Village has got two boats assigned to

it," said Bert McAlpin. "Gee, what more do
you fellows want?"

"You mean the scouts in Tent Village? I
don't know," said Danville, shrugging his
shoulders. "I'm talking about Alf's canoe.
We're not going to be in Tent Village, we're
going up on the hill; Black Hill you call it?"

"You mean Overlook Cabin?" Connie asked
in surprise.

"Mmm, soon as they clear it out for us."

"That'll cost money—twelve bucks a week
not counting board," Connie said.

"Yep, so I understand."

"The bosses will have something to say about
that."

"I've engaged it," said Danville, then he
added rather oddly: "You don't suppose I'm
not acquainted with my own father, do you?"

"Gee, that's some perch," said Connie.

"Not so bad," said Danville. "How 'bout
the key?"

"You going to take the kid up there?"

"N—no."

"Bunk up there alone?"

"No, Alf and I are going together."

"That's what I mean," said Connie.

"It isn't what you said," said Danville.
"How about the locker key? They tell me in

Administration Shack you'll have to hand it over. In fact, they wouldn't let you do this thing at all if I hadn't asked them to let us have the cabin. You can't let out a member of your patrol up here, without your scoutmaster. But as long as it's O.K. with Alf I don't suppose anybody cares; I'm sure you don't. Only if you don't let him have his prize canoe you'll get the management interested and then you won't be able to have your Eagle Scout at all. You fellows ought not to complain at handing over his canoe; you're getting an Eagle Scout.''

"Hey, Bently," said Hunt Ward in a sudden burst of familiarity; "is it true that *you're* an Eagle Scout? A lot of scouts say you are?''

"No, I'm not.''

"Nobody seems to know about you,'' Vic said.

"Tom Slade seems to think it's all right if Alf wants to go up on the hill,'' said Danville, ignoring their personal queries. "Seems to me you Elks are getting your own way pretty soft and easy. Only you'll spoil everything if you don't hand over the locker key.''

"You told—you talked to Slady?'' Connie asked.

"Oh, yes. I don't think there'll be any trouble as long as I hire the cabin and you hand over the canoe; 'long as Alf has a place to stay.''

"Did they take your word for it before hearing from your father?" Connie asked.

"Why, sure; why not?"

"Scouts can't do business with the management," Connie said.

"So? Well, I must have caught them napping, I suppose," said Bently. "How 'bout the key?"

"Here it is, tell him we wish him luck and hope he won't get drowned," said Connie.

"If he does, I'll let you know," said Danville. "And I congratulate you on getting an Eagle Scout; that's some nifty haul."

"Can you blame us?" Bert McAlpin asked.

"No, an eagle's an eagle," said Danville.

"Poor kid, he's only a little mascot," Vic said. "I haven't been up there on Black Hill since we were having signal tests last summer. Are there two bunks in the cabin? I thought there was only one."

"There are three," said Danville. "So we can each have one and a half. Well, so long."

"Gee williger, that guy has a way of managing things," said Connie. "I only hope Wainwright doesn't put the kibosh on it. Gee, if we can't get Holly now, *good night,* I'll be sore! There's only two other Eagle Patrols in camp. An eagle has got wings, and when you've got wings you can fly.''

''We'll fly all right,'' said Bert McAlpin. ''That gives us a look in on three awards, Yellowstone Park——''

''The kid will be just as happy,'' said Connie.

''Sure, he will,'' said several others in chorus.

CHAPTER XXXI

HOLLY HOLLIS

Overlook Cabin had not been built for season occupancy. It had been thrown up as a little storehouse for paraphernalia used on the hill, which was called Black Hill because it rose above a treacherous marsh and overlooked Black Lake. The reader will find helpful the accompanying rough sketch of the locality. Black Hill, as will be seen, lay to the east of the camp. The slope was gradual from the south where the highroad passed. But on reaching the brow of the hill one looked down from a dizzy precipice.

Between this precipice and the lake was a marsh about which weird stories were told, but the worst that was actually known of it was that it was the foregathering place of a choral society of frogs whose croaking made it seem weird enough at night. From the lake you could pole a boat into this marsh, but not all the way to the base of the cliff. Sometimes, after heavy or prolonged rains, the marsh would be entirely submerged, but usually it was

213

visible as a rank and vivid green area with patches of scum.

The cabin on the brow of the cliff had been built for the accommodation of certain scout activities which had been conducted there. Close to the edge was a rather odd contrivance, conspicuous from the lake below, and newcomers seldom failed to ask about its purpose, though now in its time of disuse and comparative dilapidation, few took the trouble to ascend the hill and view it at close range. This was a square wooden frame about eight or ten feet in size, standing upright and held by means of braces in the ground. It was loose and rickety from the force of heavy winds. Stretched in this was a sheet of canvas, bound to the frame with windings of light rope, by which it could be tightened. The canvas came to within a few inches of the frame all the way round.

This affair was known as a signal easel and had been used for practice in signalling. Illuminated at night by a bonfire at a safe distance in back of it the screen was as brilliant as the silver screen of the movies. Then a scout standing between it and the precipice was revealed in striking silhouette as he manipulated wigwag flags. From all the way across the lake he could be seen, a weird and vivid sight in the

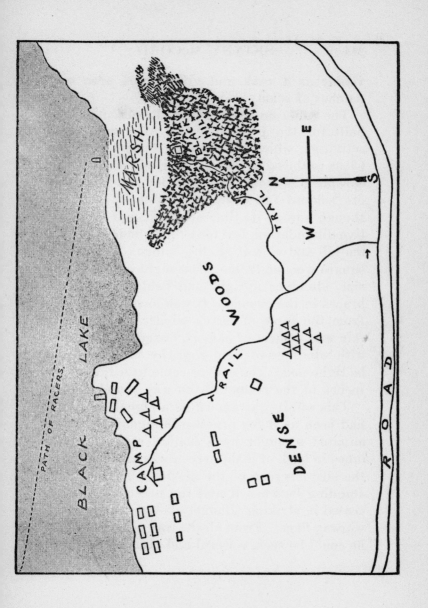

night time, and in this way codes were tried
out and practiced. Once, on a memorable occasion, that redoubtable showman, Pee-wee
Harris, had given a motion picture exhibit here
with his prize outfit at the appallingly low ad-
mission fee of ten cents. But there being no
gate, the place was overrun by deadheads and
the exhibition ended in a riot.

The cabin was filled with old signalling paraphernalia, flags and smudge buckets. It had
three bunks and some rough camping necessi-
ties used by hunters in the winter. A ghost
was also said to live there, but if so he must
have been of a retiring nature for he was never
seen. The rental charge which Connie Bennett
had mentioned was made so as to limit the use
of the place to older visitors at camp, field men
and the like. Eagle Scouts may come and go,
but it is probably true that Danville Bently was
the only boy of scouting age at camp who could
so easily have made arrangements to use the
place.

It was here that he and Skinny settled down
to a kind of frontier life, to a companionship
which Danville regarded in a humorous way,
but never so as to belittle his odd companion.
They ate down at camp, of course, and usually
attended camp-fire, but otherwise they led a life

apart, stalking, tracking and hiking about the
woods. Danville did his fourteen mile hike,
but there was no boy to train for a tenderfoot,
so there he remained for the time being; he
seemed not greatly interested in scouting progress merely for its own sake. He was easy-
going and casual, a good looker-on. He seemed
never to think about how near he had come to
wearing the Gold Cross; so far as Skinny could
see, that badge of the highest heroism meant
nothing to him. Perhaps he did not care for
things because it was so easy for him to get
them. The pomp and fuss and honors and
awards did not appeal to him.

He showed no resentment toward the Elks
for their shabby treatment of Skinny, but the
Elks knew that he had seen them at their worst
and they avoided him. Every scout in camp
felt that here was a boy of unlimited reserve
power; a boy who would never do a thing simply for a thrill or a badge, but who would prove
invincible when aroused to act for a purpose.
They all respected him and there was no hint
of banter in the nickname of *White Scarf* by
which he came to be known. That spotless
white scarf was a familiar sight in camp and
singled him out from all other scouts and made
him conspicuous.

As for the Elks, they got what they wanted and basked in the glory of it. An Eagle Scout is a wonderful thing, embodying all the heroic romance of scouting. He is a glory to his patrol. And at Temple Camp such a one was an asset to his patrol since only certain endowment rewards were open to Eagle patrols. Holly Hollis came not unheralded by his new patrol colleagues, and it must be admitted that he filled his place with a becomingness never achieved by poor little Skinny. On the evening of his arrival he attracted a good deal of attention as he passed through the "eats" pavilion with the Elks on his way to supper. A number of scouts arose and gave him the full salute, and there was a rather discordant attempt on the part of a few enthusiasts to sing

"You can't go higher than an Eagle,
    As every scout should know;
You have to stop when you get to the top,
    It's as high as you can go."

He wore his full regalia with his Eagle badge above his left breast pocket, and his sleeve was covered with his twenty-one merit badges. A slim boy he was, with very black hair and a look in his pleasant face that bespoke something rather more than powers—a touch of the venturesome. No stick-in-the-mud was this Eagle of the darting and roaming black eyes.

And those eyes did not fail to notice things, for no sooner had he taken his place at table than turning to the proud Connie he asked, "Who's that fellow over at the third table with the white scarf?"

He was to know that fellow well before his season at Temple Camp was over.

CHAPTER XXXII

Again there was great excitement around the camp-fire. Again they were making merry at the expense of Skinny. Again Skinny smiled shyly, just as he did on that night when they made such ostentatious show of helping him find his compass. Seeing him bashful and discomfited, scouts who did not even know him (for now the big camp was crowded) laughed, and added their bantering comments to the general chorus. Few knew his last name; fewer still knew his first name, or who he was or where he bunked. He was just the little camp mascot. They were talking about the Eagle race, which was one of the big events of camp, and some waggish scout had suggested Skinny to accompany one or other of the three Eagle Scouts in this contest. And another boy had scorned this suggestion, saying that Skinny was too heavy. And so on, and so on.

Each summer, at the height of the season, this gala contest was held. It was dated to occur at that time because then there were likely

to be several Eagle Scouts at camp. Eagle
Scouts are none too prevalent and if rigid test-
ing were the invariable rule, they would be even
less prevalent. It often happened that a whole
season passed at Temple Camp with only one
or two Eagles present, and these not at the
same time. Once the race (most spectacular
event of the season) had not been held because
there were no contestants. This event was the
world series of Temple Camp, establishing a
supreme hero, an Eagle Scout with a sensational triumph to top his glory. Despite the
song, one *could* get a little higher than an
Eagle, and that was by a thrilling victory over
other Eagles. Such a victor was always the
great hero of camp.

Just as no scout is eligible for merit badges
until he is in the first class, so no scout but an
Eagle of twenty-one badges was eligible to try
for this Mary Temple Cup which carried with
it a two weeks' holiday at the Grand Canyon
for the victor and his patrol. Transportation
papers were always inside the cup, a tempting
beverage indeed, proffered by the pretty hands
of the young daughter of the camp's founder.
So you can hardly blame the Elks for coveting
this prize; they were not the first in this glori-
ous republic to resort to political maneuvers

to acquire an eligible contestant. There were just three such contestants now, Howell Cross, Ellis Carway and Holly Hollis.

Everything was set for the morrow and they were making merry at the expense of Skinny. His shy smile illumined his pale, temperamental face, and his characteristic embarrassment was amusingly evident in the fitful glow of the mounting blaze.

"Hey, Howell, don't you think if Skinny took off his shoes and shirt he'd be light enough?"

"How 'bout you, Eagle Carway? Skinny means good luck. I took him on a hike and found an oriole's nest, honest. You can't lose with Skinny."

"Sure, if you should fall in a faint he'd take the oars right out of your hands and glide to victory; he wouldn't stop till he got to the Grand Canyon."

"How 'bout you, Holly? Skinny used to be an Elk, honest. But he's way above that now, he's up on Black Hill."

"Trouble with Skinny is he'd sink the boat. If he started smiling it would go right down. Why his smile alone weighs forty pounds, don't it, Skinny? What are you blushing about, Skinny? What would you do if you had to take the cup from Mary Temple?"

"Yes, and suppose she should kiss you—
good night!"

"I'm going to have Skinny root for me,"
said Eagle Scout Cross.

"Sure, the human megaphone. Stand up,
Skinny, and let the three of them draw lots for
you; don't be afraid. Who wants Skinny to
man the tiller?"

And so forth and so on. All three Eagles had
chosen their steersmen from their own patrols;
they laughed pleasantly at the idea of Skinny
as steersman of a racing shell. Holly Hollis,
who sat across the fire, made a funny grimace
at him. Danville Bently wondered how much
Hollis knew of Skinny's ups and downs in the
scouting field, and especially his fate in the
hands of his honor seeking colleagues. The
funny grimace didn't mean much.

"Never mind, Alf," said Danville as they
walked up the hill. The night seemed unusually
black after the glare of the camp-fire. "If you
help them to have fun, what more do you
want?"

"I don't mind," Skinny said. He was perfectly at ease with Danville and always talked
freely. "Even I want them to win—my patrol,
I mean. He smiled at me, that Eagle Scout, did
you see?"

"Yep, I saw."

"I can call it my patrol even now, can't I? Connie said I could."

"Sure, if you want to; 'long as I don't have to call them mine."

"Are you mad at them?"

"No, no, Alf."

"They're my patrol just like Danny is my brother, ain't they? I got to be loyal."

"Yes, sure, I understand, Alf."

"Can I help liking Danny?"

"No, I can't help liking him either. I have a sort of hunch that he could win that race if he were an Eagle."

"Then I'd have a lot of honor, hey?"

"Sure would."

"I bet you could win it, too."

"I've got my job," said Danville.

For a few minutes they walked on up the hill and neither spoke. Then, noticing that Skinny's shoulders were shaking, Danville paused abruptly. The little fellow was gulping. Danville broke his rule and called him kid.

"Alf—what's the matter, kid?" he asked feelingly. "Don't—what's the matter, Alf? Can't you tell me?"

Skinny couldn't tell him, because he didn't exactly know.

"Anyway, they were right, because I didn't have any scout suit," he sobbed.

"Well, you've got me, haven't you? Aren't you satisfied?"

"Yes, but I want them to win and go out there to the cannon,* because they're my patrol and I'm not mad at them. Only I don't want to go and see the race, because I'll get all excited like, because I want them to win. Do you think they'll win?"

"Who can tell who will win, kid? We'll stay up on the hill all by ourselves and watch it from a distance. Will that be all right?"

"Yes, but do you think they'll win?"

"I think Hollis has got the stuff in him."

"You've got to be an Eagle, haven't you?"

"Yes, but you see there are three Eagles? And we can't tell who'll be the big scream when the day is over."

No indeed, no one could tell that.

* He meant canyon.

CHAPTER XXXIII

VICTORY AND THEN——

The precipice was not a bad place from which to view the finish. It was not close enough to the excitement for most scouts, but it afforded a good gallery seat. Danville was glad that no one came up there. He had a big piece of charred wood with which he intended to mark the name of the winner in big letters on the signal canvas as soon as the race was over. Then he and Skinny would shout and draw attention to it. He hoped for Skinny's sake that the name would be Hollis.

The race, as you will see by the map, began at the northwestern end of the lake, followed a southeasterly course and ended where the shells passed an anchored skiff in which were spectators, who had a good view of the approaching shells. The lake was dotted with boats and canoes and it required a constant zigzagging about of the camp launch to keep them off the course. It was a gala scene.

After a while the launch chugged away along the course and there were fifteen or twenty

minutes of tense waiting. Soon its shrill
whistle could be heard and Skinny was trembling with excitement as it reappeared with
its *clear the way* pennant flying and its
whistle calling a warning to keep the course
clear.

Then they came in sight, the three shells, red
and shining in the bright sunlight. They
seemed to be abreast, throwing out three white
V's of light spray as on, on, on they came.
Every nerve in Skinny's little body was on
edge as he stood near the brow of the precipice
trying to identify the salmon colored pennant
of the Elks. Then he saw it—yes, he saw it.
It was one of the two shells that glided abreast;
the other had fallen behind. He could see the
form of the rower bent forward and back, the
long oars feathering, the slender shell moving
nearer, nearer, under the impetus of that
steady, increasing leverage.

The third shell, manned by Ellis Carway,
seemed now quite out of the running. Its
heroic Eagle was doing ragged and erratic
work, never getting the full benefit of his
strokes. In that short course he could never
make up what he had lost. But the other two
seemed evenly matched. Suddenly Howell
Cross's shell, with the blue pennant of his

patrol, shot ahead. Skinny trembled, his eyes
stared, he quivered with excitement.

He might have saved his fears. Howell had
his spurt, and having spent his reserve energy,
could only maintain his former speed. The
time for a spurt is at the end and Holly Hollis
knew this. Easily he shot ahead in an excess
of effort that would surely carry him past the
skiff. He would not have to pause for breath
till he could pause for good. Now he was half
a length ahead. Now a full length. And then
amid a wild chorus of cheers and the waving of
hundreds of flags, he swept forward past the
skiff. The Eagle of the Elk Patrol had won
them the cup and the trip to the Grand Canyon,
and the glory of being the banner patrol of
Temple Camp. Skinny's patrol.

Then something happened which caused Danville Bently to run along the cliff excitedly
trying to make out just what the trouble was.
There was a sudden change in the tone of the
shouting below. He came to a point where he
could descend with caution and as he did so,
he perceived the dreadful thing that had happened. Hollis had evidently turned his victorious shell quickly so that the tremendous force
of its impetus would not carry it against the
steep shore (see map) and it had swept into the

marsh and capsized. And there he was quite out of reach of it, sinking in the treacherous rank growth. Danville made out that he had tried to swim only to be caught in the mire. From where Danville was descending cautiously the victim looked like only half a boy, the upper half. He seemed standing up right in the swamp.

"Do your feet touch?" Danville heard some one call.

"Help, help!" was the frantic answer.

It had always been said that there was death in this marsh. There was a story of a duck hunter who had been swallowed up in it. If Hollis had not tried to swim and remained by his inverted shell, he would have suffered nothing worse than an inglorious climax to his spectacular triumph. But he had somehow got to the very center of the horrible place where no boat could penetrate. The excitement on the neighboring shore was frenzied. Some one tried to pole a boat into the marsh; it got stuck in the thickening growth and could not be moved either way. And meanwhile, Hollis' frantic cry for help rose as he sank lower, lower. . . .

Then suddenly a great white thing seemed to fill the sky. It tumbled, shook, like some air-

plane run amuck. And with a loud sound of
splitting wood it settled flat upon the enveloping
marsh. They saw, but they hardly knew what
they were witnessing. They stared aghast.
Then as they saw a little living form reach out
from the safe area of canvas that lay flat upon
that frightful consuming mud a cheer went up
—and another, and another, until the heavens
seemed rent with a swelling chorus of mad ac-
claim. But it was not for the victorious Eagle
they were screaming their lungs out as their
fears subsided. It was just for the little outcast scout who, in such a sublime frenzy as only
his trembling body could experience, had torn
and wrenched the signal easel from its lodg-
ment and crashed down with this spreading
parachute to the rescue of the boy who had
brought glory to the Elk Patrol.

CHAPTER XXXIV

THE PRICE

Given time they managed to get a boat in somehow, poling it this way and that and finally taking the marsh, as one might say, by flanking tactics. With the large area of resisting canvas lying upon the yielding morass, there was no great need for hurry. The frame was broken, but it could not sink. And the Eagle Scout, beneath whose weight the loosened canvas sagged, was safe. No boat could have saved him. No swimmer could have averted that imminent tragedy. But the eager-eyed little fellow who squatted there on that outlandish, sustaining rug, glancing at the Eagle Scout as if he were a god, had done it. His shirt was in shreds; a great rent in his faded trousers exposed his whole thin little leg. He did not look like a boy scout at all; you could not find a picture on all of your scout posters that bears the faintest resemblance to him.

As the boat neared the canvas a tall boy with a white scarf gently pushed a couple of scoutmasters aside and helped the bewildered Skinny

into the boat. He seemed to intimate that
Skinny belonged to him and the rest should
take notice and keep their hands off. Then he
allowed them to help Holly Hollis aboard.
And so they made slow progress out of the
dreadful place and nothing was left there but
the big broken frame with its soiled expanse of
canvas. A very big triumphant pennant for
such a little boy!

They were all crowding at the landing place
and the diving board bent dangerously under
the weight of gaping scouts. The Elks were
there. Even Chocolate Drop, the darky cook,
had come down in his white cap and apron, gaz-
ing as if he saw a ghost. And no one said a
word about the race.

"Can't I go up on the hill with you fellows?"
Holly asked.

"Sure, only you'll have to come down again,"
said Danville. "Wait till you get your bathing
trunks off and are all washed up and rested,
then come up and make us a call. Eagle Scouts
are always welcome."

But Holly Hollis shook his head and brushed
Connie Bennett aside and interrupted Vic Norris, who seemed to have something to pro-
pose.

"No, I mean to stay," said he. "You're the

ones I belong with. I resign from the Elk Patrol."

"You can't do that, you're our Eagle Scout," said Connie.

"And where would your Eagle Scout be if it wasn't for the little chap that gave his place to him, and just now risked his life to save him —*for you!*" said Danville Bently. "I don't know whether they have diamond studded crosses; all I know is that the Gold Cross isn't good enough for him. But he'll get it all right. And if your Eagle wants to come with us, why just remember that the eagle is a free bird; he flies high and goes where he pleases—he belongs up on precipices and crags, with others who jump off cliffs. Do you get that, Connie Bennett? And you're going to lose him! Look in his face—you can tell what he's thinking. I guess he never knew that he's filling Alf's place in your patrol. Tell him about it, why don't you? How about you, Holly? Do you follow the Gold Cross—or the Elk Patrol?"

"I follow the Gold Cross," said Holly. "An Eagle is nothing but a lot of merit badges."

"So that's that," said Danville Bently.

Yes, that was that. They played for big

stakes, Connie and his patrol, and they lost. They lost both the Gold Cross and the Eagle Scout. They paid the penalty. You dance and you pay the fiddler. You may have what you crave, but you pay the price. And sometimes the price is very large. You may play high for an Eagle Scout. And the Eagle Scout may bow before the Gold Cross awarded for the heroism that is made divine by the spirit of sacrifice. For it is not true, as the song says, that an Eagle is as high as you can go. You can go higher than that if there is an elemental frenzy in your soul. The price of the Gold Cross is very, very high. For you must forget yourself and then they will remember you. Even if you are a ragged little codger out of Corkscrew Alley, they will scream your praises to the sky.

An Eagle is not as high as you can go.

THE END

This Isn't All!

Would you like to know what became of the good friends you have made in this book?

Would you like to read other stories continuing their adventures and experiences, or other books quite as entertaining by the same author?

On the *reverse side* of the wrapper which comes with this book, you will find a wonderful list of stories which you can buy at the same store where you got this book.

Don't throw away the Wrapper

Use it as a handy catalog of the books you want some day to have. But in case you do mislay it, write to the Publishers for a complete catalog.

THE TOM SLADE BOOKS

By PERCY KEESE FITZHUGH

Author of "Roy Blakeley," "Pee-wee Harris," "Westy
Martin," Etc.

**Illustrated. Individual Picture Wrappers in Colors.
Every Volume Complete in Itself.**

"Let your boy grow up with Tom Slade," is a suggestion which thousands of parents have followed during the past, with the result that the TOM SLADE BOOKS are the most popular boys' books published today. They take Tom Slade through a series of typical boy adventures through his tenderfoot days as a scout, through his gallant days as an American doughboy in France, back to his old patrol and the old camp ground at Black Lake, and so on.

TOM SLADE, BOY SCOUT
TOM SLADE AT TEMPLE CAMP
TOM SLADE ON THE RIVER
TOM SLADE WITH THE COLORS
TOM SLADE ON A TRANSPORT
TOM SLADE WITH THE BOYS OVER THERE
TOM SLADE, MOTORCYCLE DISPATCH
    BEARER
TOM SLADE WITH THE FLYING CORPS
TOM SLADE AT BLACK LAKE
TOM SLADE ON MYSTERY TRAIL
TOM SLADE'S DOUBLE DARE
TOM SLADE ON OVERLOOK MOUNTAIN
TOM SLADE PICKS A WINNER
TOM SLADE AT BEAR MOUNTAIN
TOM SLADE: FOREST RANGER
TOM SLADE IN THE NORTH WOODS

GROSSET & DUNLAP, *Publishers*, NEW YORK

THE PEE-WEE HARRIS BOOKS

By PERCY KEESE FITZHUGH

Author of "Tom Slade," "Roy Blakeley," "Westy Martin," Etc.

Illustrated. Individual Picture Wrappers in Color. Every Volume Complete in Itself.

All readers of the Tom Slade and the Roy Blakeley books are acquainted with Pee-wee Harris. These stories record the true facts concerning his size (what there is of it) and his heroism (such as it is), his voice, his clothes, his appetite, his friends, his enemies, his victims. Together with the thrilling narrative of how he foiled, baffled, circumvented and triumphed over everything and everybody (except where he failed) and how even when he failed he succeeded. The whole recorded in a series of screams and told with neither muffler nor cut-out.

PEE-WEE HARRIS

PEE-WEE HARRIS ON THE TRAIL

PEE-WEE HARRIS IN CAMP

PEE-WEE HARRIS IN LUCK

PEE-WEE HARRIS ADRIFT

PEE-WEE HARRIS F. O. B. BRIDGEBORO

PEE-WEE HARRIS FIXER

PEE-WEE HARRIS: AS GOOD AS HIS WORD

PEE-WEE HARRIS: MAYOR FOR A DAY

PEE-WEE HARRIS AND THE SUNKEN TREASURE

GROSSET & DUNLAP, *Publishers,* **NEW YORK**

THE WESTY MARTIN BOOKS

By PERCY KEESE FITZHUGH
Author of the "Tom Slade" and "Roy Blakeley" Books, Etc.

**Individual Colored Wrappers. Illustrated.
Every Volume Complete in Itself.**

Westy Martin, known to every friend of Roy Blakeley, appears as the hero of adventures quite different from those in which we have seen him participate as a Scout of Bridgeboro and of Temple Camp. On his way to the Yellowstone the bigness of the vast West and the thoughts of the wild preserve that he is going to visit make him conscious of his own smallness and of the futility of "boy scouting" and woods lore in this great region. Yet he was to learn that if it had not been for his scout training he would never have been able to survive the experiences he had in these stories.

WESTY MARTIN

WESTY MARTIN IN THE YELLOWSTONE

WESTY MARTIN IN THE ROCKIES

WESTY MARTIN ON THE SANTA FE
    TRAIL

WESTY MARTIN ON THE OLD INDIAN
    TRAILS

GROSSET & DUNLAP, *Publishers,* NEW YORK

Jerry Todd and Poppy Ott Series

BY LEO EDWARDS

Durably Bound. Illustrated. Individual Colored Wrappers. Every Volume Complete in Itself.

Hundreds of thousands of boys who laughed until their sides ached over the weird and wonderful adventures of Jerry Todd and his gang demanded that Leo Edwards, the author, give them more books like the Jerry Todd stories with their belt-bursting laughs and creepy shivers. So he took Poppy Ott, Jerry Todd's bosom chum and created the Poppy Ott Series, and if such a thing could be possible—they are even more full of fun and excitement than the Jerry Todds.

THE POPPY OTT SERIES

POPPY OTT AND THE STUTTERING PARROT
POPPY OTT AND THE SEVEN LEAGUE STILTS
POPPY OTT AND THE GALLOPING SNAIL
POPPY OTT'S PEDIGREED PICKLES

THE JERRY TODD BOOKS

JERRY TODD AND THE WHISPERING MUMMY
JERRY TODD AND THE ROSE-COLORED CAT
JERRY TODD AND THE OAK ISLAND TREASURE
JERRY TODD AND THE WALTZING HEN
JERRY TODD AND THE TALKING FROG
JERRY TODD AND THE PURRING EGG
JERRY TODD IN THE WHISPERING CAVE

GROSSET & DUNLAP, *Publishers,* NEW YORK